THE DEAD
OF
WINTER

THE DEAD
OF
WINTER

TEN CLASSIC TALES FOR CHILLING NIGHTS

Edited by Cecily Gayford

Lennox Robinson · A. M. Burrage
Ruth Rendell · E. F. Benson
Arthur Conan Doyle · H. Russell Wakefield
M. R. James · Margaret Irwin
Algernon Blackwood · W. W. Jacobs

P

PROFILE BOOKS

First published in Great Britain in 2023 by
PROFILE BOOKS LTD
29 Cloth Fair
London EC1A 7JQ
www.profilebooks.com

3 5 7 9 10 8 6 4 2

Typeset in Fournier by MacGuru Ltd
Printed and bound in Great Britain by
CPI Group (UK) Ltd, Croydon CR0 4YY

A CIP catalogue record for this book is available from the British Library.

ISBN 978 1 80081 775 3
eISBN 978 1 80081 776 0

Contents

A Pair of Muddy Shoes

Lennox Robinson

I am going to try to write it down quite simply, just as it hap-pened. I shall try not to exaggerate anything.

I am twenty-two years old, my parents are dead, I have no brothers or sisters; the only near relation I have is Aunt Margaret, my father's sister. She is unmarried and lives alone in a little house in the country in the west of county Cork. She is kind to me and I often spend my holidays with her, for I am poor and have few friends.

I am a school-teacher – that is to say, I teach drawing and singing. I am a visiting teacher at two or three schools in Dublin. I make a fair income, enough for a single woman to live comfortably on, but father left debts behind him, and until these are paid off I have to live very simply. I suppose I ought to eat more and eat better food. People sometimes think I am nervous and highly strung: I look rather fragile and delicate, but really I am not. I have slender hands, with pale, tapering fingers – the sort of hands people call 'artistic'.

I hoped very much that my aunt would invite me to spend Christmas with her. I happened to have very little money; I had paid off a big debt of poor father's, and that left me very short, and I felt rather weak and ill. I didn't quite know how I'd get through the holidays unless I went down to my aunt's. However, ten days before Christmas the invitation came. You may be sure I accepted it gratefully, and when my last school broke up on the 20th I packed my trunk, gathered up the old sentimental songs Aunt Margaret likes best, and set off for Rosspatrick.

It rains a great deal in West Cork in the winter: it was raining when Aunt Margaret met me at the station. 'It's been a terrible month, Peggy,' she said, as she turned the pony's head into the long road that runs for four muddy miles from the station to Rosspatrick. 'I think it's rained every day for the last six weeks. And the storms! We lost a chimney two days ago: it came through the roof, and let the rain into the ceiling of the spare bedroom. I've had to make you up a bed in the lumber room till Jeremiah Driscoll can be got to mend the roof.'

I assured her that any place would do me; all I wanted was her society and a quiet time.

'I can guarantee you those,' she said. 'Indeed, you look tired out: you look as if you were just after a bad illness or just before one. That teaching is killing you.'

The lumber room was really very comfortable. It was a large room with two big windows; it was on the ground floor, and Aunt Margaret had never used it as a bedroom because people are often afraid of sleeping on the ground floor.

2

We stayed up very late talking over the fire. Aunt Margaret came with me to my bedroom; she stayed there for a long time, fussing about the room, hoping I'd be comfortable, pulling about the furniture, looking at the bedclothes.

At last I began to laugh at her. 'Why shouldn't I be comfortable? Think of my horrid little bedroom in Brunswick Street! What's wrong with this room?'

'Nothing – oh, nothing,' she said rather hurriedly, and kissed me and left me.

I slept very well. I never opened my eyes till the maid called me, and then after she had left me I dozed off again. I had a ridiculous dream. I dreamed I was interviewing a rich old lady: she offered me a thousand a year and comfortable rooms to live in. My only duty was to keep her clothes from moths; she had quantities of beautiful, costly clothes, and she seemed to have a terror of them being eaten by moths. I accepted her offer at once. I remember saying to her gaily, 'The work will be no trouble to me. I like killing moths.'

It was strange I should say that, because I really don't like killing moths – I hate killing anything. But my dream was easily explained, for when I woke a second later (as it seemed), I was holding a dead moth between my finger and thumb. It disgusted me just a little bit – that dead moth pressed between my fingers, but I dropped it quickly, jumped up, and dressed myself.

Aunt Margaret was in the dining room, and full of profuse and anxious inquiries about the night I had spent. I soon relieved her anxieties, and we laughed together over my dream and the new position I was going to fill. It was very wet all day and I didn't stir out of the house. I sang a great many songs, I began a pencil-drawing of my aunt – a thing I had been meaning to make for years – but I didn't feel well, I felt headachy and nervous – just from being in the house all day, I suppose. I felt the greatest disinclination to go to bed. I felt afraid, I don't know of what.

Of course I didn't say a word of this to Aunt Margaret.

That night the moment I fell asleep I began to dream. I thought I was looking down at myself from a great height. I saw myself in my nightdress crouching in a corner of the bedroom. I remember wondering why I was crouching there, and I came nearer and looked at myself again, and then I saw that it was not myself that crouched there – it was a large white cat, it was watching a mouse-hole. I was relieved and I turned away. As I did so I heard the cat spring. I started round. It had a mouse between its paws, and it looked up at me, growling as a cat does. Its face was like a woman's face – was like my face. Probably that doesn't sound at all horrible to you, but it happens that I have a deadly fear of mice. The idea of holding one between my hands, of putting my mouth to one, of – oh, I can't bear even to write it.

I think I woke screaming. I know when I came to myself I had jumped out of bed and was standing on the floor. I lit the candle and searched the room. In one corner were some boxes and trunks; there might have been a mouse-hole behind them, but I hadn't the courage to pull them out and look. I kept my candle lighted and stayed awake all night.

The next day was fine and frosty. I went for a long walk in the morning and for another in the afternoon. When bedtime came I was very tired and sleepy. I went to sleep at once and slept dreamlessly all night.

It was the next day that I noticed my hands getting queer. 'Queer' perhaps isn't the right word, for, of course, cold does roughen and coarsen the skin, and the weather was frosty enough to account for that. But it wasn't only that the skin was rough, the whole hand looked larger, stronger, not like my own hand. How ridiculous this sounds, but the whole story is ridiculous.

I remember once, when I was a child at school, putting on another girl's boots by mistake one day. I had to go about till evening in them, and I was perfectly miserable. I could not stop myself from looking at my feet, and they seemed to me to be the feet of another person. That sickened me, I don't know why. I felt a little like that now when I looked at my hands. Aunt Margaret noticed how rough and swollen they were, and she gave me cold cream, which I rubbed on them before I went to bed.

I lay awake for a long time. I was thinking of my hands. I didn't seem to be able not to think of them. They seemed to grow bigger and bigger in the darkness; they seemed monstrous hands, the hands of some horrible ape, they seemed to fill the whole room. Of course if I had struck a match and lit the candle I'd have calmed myself in a minute, but, frankly, I hadn't the courage. When I touched one hand with the other it seemed rough and hairy, like a man's.

At last I fell asleep. I dreamed that I got out of bed and opened the window. For several minutes I stood looking out. It was bright moonlight and bitterly cold. I felt a great desire to go for a walk. I dreamed that I dressed myself quickly, put on my slippers, and stepped out of the window. The frosty grass crunched under my feet. I walked, it seemed for miles,

along a road I never remember being on before. It led uphill;
I met no one as I walked.

Presently I reached the crest of the hill, and beside the
road, in the middle of a bare field, stood a large house. It was
a gaunt, three-storied building, there was an air of decay
about it. Maybe it had once been a gentleman's place, and
was now occupied by a herd. There are many places like that
in Ireland. In a window of the highest storey there was a
light. I decided I would go to the house and ask the way
home. A gate closed the grass-grown avenue from the road;
it was fastened and I could not open it, so I climbed it. It was
a high gate but I climbed it easily, and I remember thinking
in my dream, 'If this wasn't a dream I could never climb it
so easily.'

I knocked at the door, and after I had knocked again the
window of the room in which the light shone was opened,
and a voice said, 'Who's there? What do you want?'

It came from a middle-aged woman with a pale face and
dirty strands of grey hair hanging about her shoulders.

I said, 'Come down and speak to me; I want to know the
way back to Rosspatrick.'

I had to speak two or three times to her, but at last she
came down and opened the door mistrustfully. She only
opened it a few inches and barred my way. I asked her the
road home, and she gave me directions in a nervous, startled
way.

Then I dreamed that I said, 'Let me in to warm myself.'

'It's late; you should be going home.'

But I laughed, and suddenly pushed at the door with my
foot and slipped past her.

I remember she said, 'My God,' in a helpless, terrified way. It was strange that she should be frightened, and I, a young girl all alone in a strange house with a strange woman, miles from anyone I knew, should not be frightened at all. As I sat warming myself by the fire while she boiled the kettle (for I had asked for tea), and watching her timid, terrified movements, the queerness of the position struck me, and I said, laughing, 'You seem afraid of me.'

'Not at all, miss,' she replied, in a voice which almost trembled.

'You needn't be, there's not the least occasion for it,' I said, and I laid my hand on her arm.

She looked down at it as it lay there, and said again, 'Oh, my God,' and staggered back against the range.

And so for half a minute we remained. Her eyes were fixed on my hand which lay on my lap; it seemed she could never take them off it.

'What is it?' I said.

'You've the face of a girl,' she whispered, 'and – God help me – the hands of a man.'

I looked down at my hands. They were large, strong and sinewy, covered with coarse red hairs. Strange to say they no longer disgusted me: I was proud of them – proud of their strength, the power that lay in them.

'Why should they make you afraid,' I asked. 'They are fine hands. Strong hands.'

But she only went on staring at them in a hopeless, frozen way.

'Have you ever seen such strong hands before?' I smiled at her.

'They're – they're Ned's hands,' she said at last, speaking in a whisper.

She put her own hand to her throat as if she were choking, and the fastening of her blouse gave way. It fell open. She had a long throat; it was moving as if she were finding it difficult to swallow; I wondered whether my hands would go round it.

Suddenly I knew they would, and I knew why my hands were large and sinewy, I knew why power had been given to them. I got up and caught her by the throat. She struggled so feebly; slipped down, striking her head against the range; slipped down onto the red-tiled floor and lay quite still, but her throat still moved under my hand and I never loosened my grasp.

And presently, kneeling over her, I lifted her head and bumped it gently against the flags of the floor. I did this again and again; lifting it higher, and striking it harder and harder, until it was crushed in like an egg, and she lay still. She was choked and dead.

And I left her lying there and ran from the house, and as I stepped onto the road I felt rain in my face. The thaw had come.

When I woke it was morning. Little by little my dream came back and filled me with horror. I looked at my hands. They were so tender and pale and feeble. I lifted them to my mouth and kissed them.

But when Mary called me half an hour later she broke into a long, excited story of a woman who had been murdered the night before, how the postman had found the door open and the dead body. 'And sure, miss, it was here she used to live long ago; she was near murdered once, by her husband, in this very room; he tried to choke her, she was half killed – that's why the mistress made it a lumber room. They put him in the asylum afterwards; a month ago he died there I heard.'

My mother was Scotch, and claimed she had the gift of prevision. It was evident she had bequeathed it to me. I was enormously excited. I sat up in bed and told Mary my dream.

She was not very interested, people seldom are in other people's dreams. Besides, she wanted, I suppose, to tell her news to Aunt Margaret. She hurried away. I lay in bed and thought it all over. I almost laughed, it was so strange and fantastic.

But when I got out of bed I stumbled over something. It was a little muddy shoe. At first I hardly recognised it, then I saw it was one of a pair of evening shoes I had; the other shoe lay near it. They were a pretty little pair of dark blue satin shoes, they were a present to me from a girl I loved very much, she had given them to me only a week ago.

Last night they had been so fresh and new and smart. Now they were scratched, the satin cut, and they were covered with mud. Someone had walked miles in them.

And I remembered in my dream how I had searched for my shoes and put them on.

Sitting on the bed, feeling suddenly sick and dizzy, holding the muddy shoes in my hand, I had in a blinding instant a vision of a red-haired man who lay in this room night after night for years, hating a sleeping white-faced woman who lay beside him, longing for strength and courage to choke her. I saw him come back, years afterwards – freed by death – to this room; saw him seize on a feeble girl too weak to resist him; saw him try her, strengthen her hands, and at last – through her – accomplish his unfinished deed … The vision passed all in a flash as it had come. I pulled myself together. 'That is nonsense, impossible,' I told myself. 'The murderer will be found before evening.'

But in my hand I still held the muddy shoes. I seem to be holding them ever since.

Smee

A. M. Burrage

'No,' said Jackson, with a deprecatory smile, 'I'm sorry. I don't want to upset your game. I shan't be doing that because you'll have plenty without me. But I'm not playing any games of hide-and-seek.'

It was Christmas Eve, and we were a party of fourteen with just the proper leavening of youth. We had dined well; it was the season for childish games, and we were all in the mood for playing them – all, that is, except Jackson. When somebody suggested hide-and-seek there was rapturous and almost unanimous approval. His was the one dissentient voice.

It was not like Jackson to spoil sport or refuse to do as others wanted. Somebody asked him if he were feeling seedy.

'No,' he answered. 'I feel perfectly fit, thanks. But,' he added with a smile which softened without retracting the flat refusal, 'I'm not playing hide-and-seek.'

One of us asked him why not. He hesitated for some seconds before replying.

'I sometimes go and stay at a house where a girl was killed through playing hide-and-seek in the dark. She didn't know the house very well. There was a servant's staircase with a door to it. When she was pursued she opened the door and jumped into what she must have thought was one of the bed-rooms – and she broke her neck at the bottom of the stairs.'

We all looked concerned, and Mrs Fernley said:

'How awful! And you were there when it happened?'

Jackson shook his head very gravely. 'No,' he said, 'but I was there when something else happened. Something worse.'

'I shouldn't have thought anything could be worse.'

'This was,' said Jackson, and shuddered visibly. 'Or so it seemed to me.'

I think he wanted to tell the story and was angling for encouragement. A few requests which may have seemed to him to lack urgency, he affected to ignore and went off at a tangent.

'I wonder if any of you have played a game called "Smee". It's a great improvement on the ordinary game of hide-and-seek. The name derives from the ungrammatical colloquialism, "It's me." You might care to play if you're going to play a game of that sort. Let me tell you the rules.

'Every player is presented with a sheet of paper. All the sheets are blank except one, on which is written "Smee". Nobody knows who is "Smee" except "Smee" himself – or herself, as the case may be. The lights are then turned out and "Smee" slips from the room and goes off to hide, and after an interval the other players go off in search, without knowing whom they are actually in search of. One player meeting another challenges with the word "Smee" and the other player, if not the one concerned, answers "Smee".

'The real "Smee" makes no answer when challenged, and the second player remains quietly by him. Presently they will be discovered by a third player, who, having challenged and received no answer, will link up with the first two. This goes on until all the players have formed a chain, and the last to join is marked down for a forfeit. It's a good noisy, romping game, and in a big house it often takes a long time to complete the chain. You might care to try it; and I'll pay my forfeit and smoke one of Tim's excellent cigars here by the fire until you get tired of it.'

I remarked that it sounded a good game and asked Jackson if he had played it himself.

'Yes,' he answered; 'I played it in the house I was telling you about.'

'And *she* was there? The girl who broke—'

'No, no,' Mrs Fernley interrupted. 'He told us he wasn't there when it happened.'

Jackson considered. 'I don't know if she was there or not. I'm afraid she was. I know that there were thirteen of us and there ought only to have been twelve. And I'll swear that I didn't know her name, or I think I should have gone clean off my head when I heard that whisper in the dark. No, you don't catch me playing that game, or any other like it, anymore. It spoiled my nerve for quite a while, and I can't afford to take long holidays. Besides, it saves a lot of trouble and inconvenience to own up at once to being a coward.'

Tim Vouce, the best of hosts, smiled around at us, and in

that smile there was a meaning which is sometimes vulgarly expressed by the slow closing of an eye. 'There's a story coming,' he announced.

'There's certainly a story of sorts,' said Jackson, 'but whether it's coming or not—' He paused and shrugged his shoulders.

'Well, you're going to pay a forfeit instead of playing?'

'Please. But have a heart and let me down lightly. It's not just a sheer cussedness on my part.'

'Payment in advance,' said Tim, 'insures honesty and promotes good feeling. You are therefore sentenced to tell the story here and now.'

And here follows Jackson's story, unrevised by me and passed on without comment to a wider public.

Some of you, I know, have run across the Sangstons. Christopher Sangston and his wife, I mean. They're distant connections of mine – at least, Violet Sangston is. About eight years ago they bought a house between the North and South Downs on the Surrey and Sussex border, and five years ago they invited me to come and spend Christmas with them.

It was a fairly old house – I couldn't say exactly of what period – and it certainly deserved the epithet 'rambling'. It wasn't a particularly big house, but the original architect, whoever he may have been, had not concerned himself with economising in space, and at first you could get lost in it quite easily.

Well, I went down for that Christmas, assured by Violet's letter that I knew most of my fellow guests and that the two or three who might be strangers to me were all 'lambs'.

Unfortunately, I'm one of the world's workers, and I couldn't get away until Christmas Eve, although the other members of the party had assembled on the preceding day. Even then I had to cut it rather fine to be there for dinner on my first night. They were all dressing when I arrived and I had to go straight to my room and waste no time. I may even have kept dinner waiting a bit, for I was last down, and it was announced within a minute of my entering the drawing room. There was just time to say 'hullo' to everybody I knew, to be briefly introduced to the two or three I didn't know, and then I had to give my arm to Mrs Gorman.

I mention this as the reason why I didn't catch the name of a tall, dark, handsome girl I hadn't met before. Everything was rather hurried and I am always bad at catching people's names. She looked cold and clever and rather forbidding, the sort of girl who gives the impression of knowing all about men and the more she knows of them the less she likes them. I felt that I wasn't going to hit it off with this particular 'lamb' of Violet's, but she looked interesting all the same, and I wondered who she was. I didn't ask, because I was pretty sure of hearing somebody address her by name before very long.

Unluckily, though, I was a long way off her at table, and as Mrs Gorman was at the top of her form that night I soon forgot to worry about who she might be. Mrs Gorman is one of the most amusing women I know, an outrageous but quite innocent flirt, with a very sprightly wit which isn't always unkind. She can think half a dozen moves ahead in conversation just as an expert can in a game of chess. We were soon sparring, or, rather, I was 'covering' against the ropes, and I quite forgot to ask her in an undertone the name of the cold, proud beauty. The lady on the other side of me was a stranger, or had been until a few minutes since, and I didn't think of seeking information in that quarter.

There was a round dozen of us, including the Sangstons themselves, and we were all young or trying to be. The Sangstons themselves were the oldest members of the party and their son Reggie, in his last year at Marlborough, must have been the youngest. When there was talk of playing games after dinner it was he who suggested 'Smee'. He told us how to play it just as I've described it to you.

His father chipped in as soon as we all understood what was going to be required of us. 'If there are any games of that sort going on in the house,' he said, 'for goodness' sake be careful of the back stairs on the first-floor landing. There's a door to them and I've often meant to take it down. In the dark anybody who doesn't know the house very well might think they were walking into a room. A girl actually did break her neck on those stairs about ten years ago when the Ainsties lived here.'

I asked how it happened.

'Oh,' said Sangston, 'there was a party here one Christmas time and they were playing hide-and-seek as you propose doing. This girl was one of the hiders. She heard somebody coming, ran along the passage to get away, and opened the door of what she thought was a bedroom, evidently with the intention of hiding behind it while her pursuer went past. Unfortunately it was the door leading to the back stairs, and that staircase is as straight and almost as steep as the shaft of a pit. She was dead when they picked her up.'

We all promised for our own sakes to be careful. Mrs Gorman said that she was sure nothing could happen to her, since she was insured by three different firms, and her next-of-kin was a brother whose consistent ill-luck was a byword in the family. You see, none of us had known the unfortunate girl, and as the tragedy was ten years old there was no need to pull long faces about it.

Well, we started the game almost immediately after dinner. The men allowed themselves only five minutes before joining the ladies, and then young Reggie Sangston went round and assured himself that the lights were out all over the house except in the servants' quarters and in the drawing room where we were assembled. We then got busy with twelve sheets of paper which he twisted into pellets and shook up between his hands before passing them round. Eleven of them were blank, and 'Smee' was written on the twelfth. The person drawing the latter was the one who had to hide. I looked and saw that mine was a blank. A moment later out went the electric lights, and in the darkness I heard somebody get up and creep to the door.

After a minute or so somebody gave a signal and we made a rush for the door. I for one hadn't the least idea which of the party was 'Smee'. For five or ten minutes we were all rushing up and down passages and in and out of rooms challenging one another and answering, '*Smee? – Smee!*'

After a bit the alarums and excursions died down, and I guessed that 'Smee' was found. Eventually I found a chain of people all sitting still and holding their breath on some narrow stairs leading up to a row of attics. I hastily joined it, having challenged and been answered with silence, and presently two more stragglers arrived, each racing the other to avoid being last. Sangston was one of them, indeed it was he who was marked down for a forfeit, and after a little while he remarked in an undertone, 'I think we're all here now, aren't we?'

He struck a match, looked up the shaft of the staircase, and began to count. It wasn't hard, although we just about filled the staircase, for we were sitting each a step or two above the next, and all our heads were visible.

'… nine, ten, eleven, twelve – *thirteen*,' he concluded, and then laughed. 'Dash it all, that's one too many!'

The match had burned out and he struck another and began to count. He got as far as twelve, and then uttered an exclamation.

'There are thirteen people here!' he exclaimed. 'I haven't counted myself yet.'

'Oh, nonsense!' I laughed. 'You probably began with yourself, and now you want to count yourself twice.'

Out came his son's electric torch, giving a brighter and steadier light and we all began to count. Of course we numbered twelve.

Sangston laughed.

'Well,' he said, 'I could have sworn I counted thirteen twice.'

From halfway up the stairs came Violet Sangston's voice with a little nervous trill in it. 'I thought there was somebody sitting two steps above me. Have you moved up, Captain Ransome?'

Ransome said that he hadn't: he also said that he thought there was somebody sitting between Violet and himself.

Just for a moment there was an uncomfortable Something in the air, a little cold ripple which touched us all. For that little moment it seemed to all of us, I think, that something odd and unpleasant had happened and was liable to happen again. Then we laughed at ourselves and at one another and were comfortable once more. There *were* only twelve of us, and there *could* only have been twelve of us, and there was no argument about it. Still laughing we trooped back to the drawing room to begin again.

This time I was 'Smee', and Violet Sangston ran me to earth while I was still looking for a hiding place. That round didn't last long, and we were a chain of twelve within two or three minutes. Afterwards there was a short interval. Violet wanted a wrap fetched for her, and her husband went up to get it from her room. He was no sooner gone than Reggie pulled me by the sleeve. I saw that he was looking pale and sick.

'Quick!' he whispered, 'while father's out of the way. Take me into the smoke room and give me a brandy or a whisky or something.'

Outside the room I asked him what was the matter, but he didn't answer at first, and I thought it better to dose him first and question him afterward. So I mixed him a pretty dark-complexioned brandy and soda which he drank at a gulp and then began to puff as if he had been running.

'I've had rather a turn,' he said to me with a sheepish grin.

'What's the matter?'

'I don't know. You were "Smee" just now, weren't you? Well, of course I didn't know who "Smee" was, and while mother and the others ran into the west wing and found you, I turned east. There's a deep clothes cupboard in my bedroom – I'd marked it down as a good place to hide when it was my turn, and I had an idea that "Smee" might be there. I opened the door in the dark, felt round, and touched somebody's hand. "Smee?" I whispered, and not getting any answer I thought I had found "Smee".

'Well, I don't know how it was, but an odd creepy feeling came over me, I can't describe it, but I felt that something was wrong. So I turned on my electric torch and there was nobody there. Now, I swear I touched a hand, and I was filling up the doorway of the cupboard at the time, so nobody could get out and past me.' He puffed again. 'What do you make of it?' he asked.

'You imagined that you had touched a hand,' I answered, naturally enough.

He uttered a short laugh. 'Of course I knew you were going to say that,' he said. 'I must have imagined it, mustn't I?' He paused and swallowed. 'I mean, it couldn't have been anything else *but* imagination, could it?'

I assured him that it couldn't, meaning what I said, and he accepted this, but rather with the philosophy of one who knows he is right but doesn't expect to be believed. We returned together to the drawing room where, by that time, they were all waiting for us and ready to start again.

It may have been my imagination – although I'm almost sure it wasn't – but it seemed to me that all enthusiasm for the game had suddenly melted like a white frost in strong sunlight. If anybody had suggested another game I'm sure we should all have been grateful and abandoned 'Smee'. Only nobody did. Nobody seemed to like to. I for one, and I can speak for some of the others too, was oppressed with the feeling that there was something wrong. I couldn't have said what I thought was wrong, indeed I didn't think about it at all, but somehow all the sparkle had gone out of the fun, and hovering over my mind like a shadow was the warning of some sixth sense which told me that there was an influence in the house which was neither sane, sound nor healthy. Why did I feel like that? Because Sangston had counted thirteen of us instead of twelve, and his son had thought he had touched somebody in an empty cupboard. No, there was more in it than just that. One would have laughed at such things in the ordinary way, and it was just that feeling of something being wrong which stopped me from laughing.

Well, we started again, and when we went in pursuit of the unknown 'Smee', we were as noisy as ever, but it seemed to me that most of us were acting. Frankly, for no reason other than the one I've given you, we'd stopped enjoying the game. I had an instinct to hunt with the main pack, but after a few minutes, during which no 'Smee' had been found, my instinct to play winning games and be first if possible, set me searching on my own account. And on the first floor of the west wing following the wall which was actually the shell of the house, I blundered against a pair of human knees.

I put out my hand and touched a soft, heavy curtain. Then I knew where I was. There were tall, deeply recessed windows with seats along the landing, and curtains over the recesses to the ground. Somebody was sitting in a corner of this window seat behind the curtain. Aha, I had caught 'Smee'! So I drew the curtain aside, stepped in, and touched the bare arm of a woman.

It was a dark night outside, and, moreover, the window was not only curtained but a blind hung down to where the bottom panes joined up with the frame. Between the curtain and the window it was as dark as the plague of Egypt. I could not have seen my hand held six inches before my face, much less the woman sitting in the corner.

'Smee?' I whispered.

I had no answer. 'Smee' when challenged does not answer. So I sat down beside her, first in the field, to await the others. Then, having settled myself I leaned over to her and whispered:

'Who is it? What's your name, "Smee"?'

And out of the darkness beside me the whisper came back: 'Brenda Ford.'

I didn't know the name, but because I didn't know it I guessed at once who she was. The tall, pale, dark girl was the only person in the house I didn't know by name. Ergo my companion was the tall, pale, dark girl. It seemed rather intriguing to be there with her, shut in between a heavy curtain and a window, and I rather wondered whether she was enjoying the game we were all playing. Somehow she hadn't seemed to me to be one of the romping sort. I muttered one or two commonplace questions to her and had no answer.

'Smee' is a game of silence. 'Smee' and the person or persons who have found 'Smee' are supposed to keep quiet to make it hard for the others. But there was nobody else about, and it occurred to me that she was playing the game a little too much to the letter. I spoke again and got no answer, and then I began to be annoyed. She was of that cold, 'superior' type which affects to despise men; she didn't like me; and she was sheltering behind the rules of a game for children to be discourteous. Well, if she didn't like sitting there with me, I certainly didn't want to be sitting there with her! I half turned from her and began to hope that we should both be discovered without much more delay.

Having discovered that I didn't like being there alone with her, it was queer how soon I found myself hating it, and that for a reason very different from the one which had at first whetted my annoyance. The girl I had met for the first time before dinner, and seen diagonally across the table, had a sort of cold charm about her which had attracted while it had half angered me. For the girl who was with me, imprisoned in the opaque darkness between the curtain and the window, I felt no attraction at all. It was so very much the reverse that I should have wondered at myself if, after the first shock of the discovery that she had suddenly become repellent to me, I had no room in my mind for anything besides the consciousness that her close presence was an increasing horror to me.

It came upon me just as quickly as I've uttered the words. My flesh suddenly shrank from her as you see a strip of gelatine shrink and wither before the heat of a fire. That feeling of something being wrong had come back to me, but multiplied to an extent which turned foreboding into actual terror. I firmly believe that I should have got up and run if I had not felt that at my first movement she would have divined my intention and compelled me to stay, by some means of which I could not bear to think. The memory of having touched her bare arm made me wince and draw in my lips. I prayed that somebody else would come along soon.

My prayer was answered. Light footfalls sounded on the

landing. Somebody on the other side of the curtain brushed against my knees. The curtain was drawn aside and a woman's hand, fumbling in the darkness, presently rested on my shoulder. 'Smee?' whispered a voice which I instantly recognised as Mrs Gorman's.

Of course she received no answer. She came and settled down beside me with a rustle, and I can't describe the sense of relief she brought me.

'It's Tony, isn't it?' she whispered.

'Yes,' I whispered back.

'You're not "Smee" are you?'

'No, she's on my other side.'

She reached a hand across me, and I heard one of her nails scratch the surface of a woman's silk gown.

'Hullo, "Smee"! How are you? Who are you? Oh, is it against the rules to talk? Never mind, Tony, we'll break the rules. Do you know, Tony, this game is beginning to irk me a little. I hope they're not going to run it to death by playing it all the evening. I'd like to play some game where we can all be together in the same room with a nice bright fire.'

'Same here,' I agreed fervently.

'Can't you suggest something when we go down? There's something rather uncanny in this particular amusement. I can't quite shed the delusion that there's somebody in this game who oughtn't to be in it at all.'

That was just how I had been feeling, but I didn't say so. But for my part the worst of my qualms were now gone; the arrival of Mrs Gorman had dissipated them. We sat on talking, wondering from time to time when the rest of the party would arrive.

I don't know how long elapsed before we heard a clatter of feet on the landing and young Reggie's voice shouting, 'Hullo! Hullo, there! Anybody there?'

'Yes,' I answered.

'Mrs Gorman with you?'

'Yes.'

'Well, you're a nice pair! You've both forfeited. We've all been waiting for you for hours.'

'Why, you haven't found "Smee" yet,' I objected.

'*You* haven't, you mean. I happen to have been "Smee" myself.'

'But "Smee's" here with us,' I cried.

'Yes,' agreed Mrs Gorman.

The curtain was stripped aside and in a moment we were blinking into the eye of Reggie's electric torch. I looked at Mrs Gorman and then on my other side. Between me and the wall there was an empty space on the window seat. I stood up at once and wished I hadn't, for I found myself sick and dizzy.

'There *was* somebody there,' I maintained, 'because I touched her.'

'So did I,' said Mrs Gorman in a voice which had lost its steadiness. 'And I don't see how she could have got up and gone without our knowing it.'

Reggie uttered a queer, shaken laugh. He, too, had had an unpleasant experience that evening. 'Somebody's been playing the goat,' he remarked. 'Coming down?'

We were not very popular when we arrived in the drawing room. Reggie rather tactlessly gave it out that he had found us sitting on a window seat behind a curtain. I taxed the tall, dark girl with having pretended to be 'Smee' and afterwards slipping away. She denied it. After which we settled down and played other games. 'Smee' was done with for the evening, and I for one was glad of it.

Some long while later, during an interval, Sangston told me, if I wanted a drink, to go into the smoke room and help myself. I went, and he presently followed me. I could see that he was rather peeved with me, and the reason came out during the following minute or two. It seemed that, in his opinion, if I must sit out and flirt with Mrs Gorman – in circumstances which would have been considered highly compromising in his young days – I needn't do it during a round game and keep everybody waiting for us.

'But there was somebody else there,' I protested, 'somebody pretending to be "Smee". I believe it was that tall, dark girl, Miss Ford, although she denied it. She even whispered her name to me.'

Sangston stared at me and nearly dropped his glass.

'Miss *Who*?' he shouted.

'Brenda Ford – she told me her name was.'

Sangston put down his glass and laid a hand on my shoulder.

'Look here, old man,' he said, 'I don't mind a joke, but don't let it go too far. We don't want all the women in the house getting hysterical. Brenda Ford is the name of the girl who broke her neck on the stairs playing hide-and-seek here ten years ago.'

A Bad Heart

Ruth Rendell

They had been very pressing and at last, on the third time of asking, he had accepted. Resignedly, almost fatalistically, he had agreed to dine with them. But as he began the long drive out of London, he thought petulantly that they ought to have had the tact to drop the acquaintance altogether. No other employee he had sacked had ever made such approaches to him. Threats, yes. Several had threatened him and one had tried blackmail, but no one had ever had the effrontery to invite him to dinner. It wasn't done. A discreet man wouldn't have done it. But of course Hugo Crouch wasn't a discreet man and that, among other things, was why he had been sacked.

He knew why they had asked him. They wanted to hold a court of enquiry, to have the whole thing out. Knowing this, he had suggested they meet in a restaurant and at his expense. They couldn't harangue a man in a public restaurant and he wouldn't be at their mercy. But they had insisted he come to their house and in the end he had given way. He was an elderly man with a heart condition; it was sixteen miles slow driving from his flat to their house – monstrous on a filthy February night – but he would show them he could take it, he would be one too many for them. The chairman of Frasers would show them he wasn't to be intimidated by a bumptious do-gooder like Hugo Crouch, and he would cope with the situation just as he had coped in the past with the blackmailer.

By the time he reached the outskirts of the Forest the rain was coming down so hard that he had to put his windscreen wipers on at full speed, and he felt more than ever thankful that he had got his new car with all its efficient gadgets. Certainly, the firm wouldn't have been able to run to it if he had kept Hugo Crouch on a day longer. If he had agreed to all Hugo's demands, he would still be stuck with that old Daimler and he would never have managed that winter cruise. Hugo had been a real thorn in his flesh what with his extravagance and his choosing to live in a house in the middle of Epping Forest. And it was in the middle, totally isolated, not even on the edge of one of the Forest villages. The general manager of Frasers had to be within reach, on call. Burying oneself out here was ridiculous.

The car's powerful headlights showed a dark winding lane ahead, the grey tree trunks making it appear like some sombre pillared corridor. And this picture was cut off every few seconds by a curtain of rain, to reappear with the sweep of the wipers. Fortunately, he had been there once before, otherwise he might have passed the high brick wall and the wooden gates behind which stood the Crouch house, the peak-roofed Victorian villa, drab, shabby, and to his eyes quite hideous. Anyone who put a demolition order on that would be doing a service to the environment, he thought, and then he drove in through the gates.

There wasn't a single light showing. He remembered that they lived in the back, but they might have put a light on to greet him. But for his car headlamps, he wouldn't have been able to see his way at all. Clutching the box of peppermint creams he had bought for Elizabeth Crouch, he splashed across the almost flooded paving, under eaves from which water poured as from a row of taps, and made for the front door which happened to be – which *would* be – at the far side of the house. It was hard to tell where their garden ended and the Forest began, for no demarcation was visible. Nothing was visible but black rain-lashed branches faintly illuminated by a dim glow showing through the fanlight over the door.

He rang the bell hard, keeping his finger on the push, hoping the rain hadn't got through his coat to his hundred-guinea suit. A jet of water struck the back of his neck, sending a shiver right through him, and then the door was opened.

'Duncan! You must be soaked. Have you had a dreadful journey?'

He gasped out, 'Awful, awful!' and ducked into the dry sanctuary of the hall. 'What a night!' He thrust the chocolates at her, gave her his hand. Then he remembered that in the old days they always used to kiss. Well, he never minded kissing a pretty woman and it hadn't been her fault. 'How are you, Elizabeth?' he said after their cheeks had touched.

'I'm fine. Let me take your coat. I'll take it into the kitchen and dry it. Hugo's in the sitting room. You know your way, don't you?'

Down a long passage, he remembered, that was never properly lighted and wasn't heated at all. The whole place cried out for central heating. He was by now extremely cold and he couldn't help thinking of his flat where the radiators got so hot that you had to open the windows even in February and where, had he been at home, his housekeeper would at this moment be placing before him a portion of hot pâté to be followed by *Poulet San Josef.* Elizabeth Crouch, he recalled, was rather a poor cook.

Outside the sitting room door he paused, girding himself for the encounter. He hadn't set eyes on Hugo Crouch since the man had marched out of the office in a huff because he, Duncan Fraser, chairman of Frasers, had tentatively suggested he might be happier in another job. Well, the sooner the first words were over the better. Very few men in his position, he thought, would let the matter weigh on their minds at all or have his sensitivity. Very few, for that matter, would have come.

He would be genial, casual, perhaps a little avuncular. Above all, he would avoid at any cost the subject of Hugo's dismissal. They wouldn't be able to make him talk about it if he was determined not to; ultimately, the politeness of hosts to guest would put up a barrier to stop them. He opened the door, smiling pleasantly, achieving a merry twinkle in his eye. 'Well, here I am, Hugo! I've made it.'

Hugo wore a very sour look, the kind of look Duncan had often seen on his face when some more than usually extravagant order or request of his had been countermanded. He didn't smile. He gave Duncan his hand gravely and asked him what he would like to drink.

Duncan looked quickly around the room, which hadn't changed and was still furnished with rather grim Victorian pieces. There was, at any rate, a huge fire of logs burning in the grate. 'Ah, yes, a drink,' he said, rubbing his hands together. He didn't dare ask for whisky, which he would have liked best, because his doctor had forbidden it. 'A little dry Vermouth?'

'I'm afraid I don't have any Vermouth.'

This rejoinder, though spoken quite lightly, though he had even expected something of the sort, gave Duncan a slight shock. It put him on his mettle and yet it jolted him. He had known, of course, that they would start on him, but he hadn't anticipated the first move coming so promptly. All right, let the man remind him he couldn't afford fancy drinks because he had lost his job. He, Duncan, wouldn't be drawn. 'Sherry, then,' he said. 'You do have sherry?'

'Oh, yes, we have sherry.' Hugo said. 'Come and sit by the fire.'

As soon as he was seated in front of those blazing logs and had begun to thaw out, he decided to pursue the conversation along the lines of the weather. It was the only subject he could think of to break the ice until Elizabeth came in, and they were doing quite well at it, moving into such sidelines as floods in East Anglia and crashes in motorway fog, when she appeared and sat next to him.

'We haven't asked anyone else, Duncan. We wanted to have you to ourselves.'

A pointless remark, he thought, under the circumstances.

Naturally, they hadn't asked anyone else. The presence of other guests would have defeated the exercise. But perhaps it hadn't been so pointless, after all. It could be an opening gambit.

'Delightful,' he said.

'We've got such a lot to talk about. I thought it would be nicer this way.'

'Much nicer.' Such a lot to talk about? There was only one thing she could mean by that. But she needn't think – silent Hugo sitting there with his grim moody face needn't think – that he would help them along an inch of the way. If they were going to get on to the subject they would have to do all the spadework themselves. 'We were just saying,' he said, 'how tragic all these motorway crashes are. Now I feel all this could be stopped by a very simple method.' He outlined the simple method, but he could tell they weren't really interested and he wasn't surprised when Elizabeth said:

'That's fascinating, Duncan, but let's talk about you. What have you been doing lately?'

Controlling the business your husband nearly ruined.

'Oh, this and that,' he said. 'Nothing much.'

'Did you go on a cruise this winter?'

'Er – yes, yes, I did. The Caribbean, as a matter of fact.'

'That's nice. I'm sure the change did you good.'

Implying he needed having good done to him, of course. She had only got on to cruises so that she could point out that some people couldn't afford them. 'I had a real rest,' he said heartily. 'I must just tell you about a most amusing thing that happened to me on the way home.' He told them, but it didn't sound very amusing and although Elizabeth smiled half-heartedly, Hugo didn't. 'Well, it seemed funny at the time,' he said.

'We can eat in five minutes,' said Elizabeth. 'Tell me, Duncan, did you buy that villa you were so keen on in the South of France?'

'Oh, yes, I bought it.' She was looking at him very curiously, very impertinently really – waiting for him to apologise for spending his own money, he supposed. 'Listen to that rain,' he said. 'It hasn't let up at all.'

They agreed that it hadn't and silence fell. He could tell from the glance they exchanged – he was very astute in these matters – that they knew they had been baulked for the time being. And they both looked pretty fed up, he thought triumphantly. But the woman was weighing in again, and a bit nearer the bone this time.

'Who do you think we ran into last week, Duncan? John Churchouse.'

The man who had done that printing for Frasers a couple of years back. He had got the order, Duncan remembered, just about the time of Hugo's promotion. He sat tight, drank the last of his sherry.

'He told us he'd been in hospital for months and lost quite a lot of business. I felt so …'

'I wonder if I might wash my hands?' Duncan asked firmly. 'If you could just tell me where the bathroom is?'

'Of course.' She looked disappointed, as well she might. 'It's the door facing you at the top of the stairs.'

Duncan made his way to the bathroom. He mustn't think he was going to get off the hook as easily as that. They would be bound to start on him again during the meal. Very likely they thought a dinner table a good place to hold an inquest. Still, he'd be ready for them, he'd done rather well up to now.

They were both waiting for him at the foot of the stairs to lead him into the dining room, and again he saw the woman give her husband one of those looks that are the equivalent of prompting nudges. Hugo was probably getting cold feet. In these cases, of course, it was always the women who were more aggressive. Duncan gave a swift glance at the table and the plate of hors d'oeuvres, sardines and anchovies and artichoke hearts, most unsuitable for the time of year.

'I'm afraid you've been to a great deal of trouble, Elizabeth,' he said graciously.

She gave him a dazzling smile. He had forgotten that smile of hers, how it lit her whole face, her eyes as flashing blue as a kingfisher's plumage. '"The labour we delight in,"' she said, '"physics pain."'

'Ah, *Macbeth*.' Good, an excellent topic to get them through the first course. 'Do you know, the only time we three ever went to the theatre together was to see *Macbeth*?'

'I remember,' she said. 'Bread, Duncan?'

'Thank you. I saw a splendid performance of *Macbeth* by that Polish company last week. Perhaps you've seen it?'

'We haven't been to the theatre at all this winter,' said Hugo.

She must have kicked him under the table to prompt that one.

Duncan took no notice. He told them in detail about the Polish *Macbeth*, although such was his mounting tenseness that he couldn't remember the names of half the characters or, for that matter, the names of the actors.

'I wish Keith could have seen it,' she said. 'It's his set play for his exam.'

She was going to force him to ask after her sons and be told they'd had to take them away from that absurdly expensive boarding school. Well, he wouldn't. Rude it might be, but he wouldn't ask.

'I don't think you ever met our children, Duncan?'

'No, I didn't.'

'They'll be home on half-term next week. I'm so delighted that their half-term happens to coincide with mine.'

'Yours?' he said suspiciously.

'Elizabeth has gone back to teaching.'

'Really?' said Duncan. 'No, I won't have any more, thank you. That was delicious. Let me give you a hand. If I could carry something …?'

'Please don't trouble. I can manage.' She looked rather offended. 'If you two will excuse me I'll see to our main course.'

He was left alone with Hugo in the chilly dining room. He shifted his legs from under the cloth to bring them closer to the one-bar electric heater. Hugo began to struggle with the cork of a wine bottle. Unable to extract it, he cursed under his breath.

'Let me try.'

'I'll be able to cope quite well, thanks, if you don't watch me,' said Hugo sharply, and then, irrelevantly, if you didn't know nothing those two said was irrelevant, 'I'm doing a course in accountancy.'

'As a wine waiter, Hugo,' said Duncan, 'you make a very good accountant, ha ha!'

Hugo didn't laugh. He got the cork out at last. 'I think I'll do all right. I was always reasonably good at figures.'

'So you were, so you were. And more than reasonably good.' That was true. It had been with personnel that the man was so abysmally bad, giving junior executives and little typists ideas above their station. 'I'm sure you'll do well.'

Why didn't the woman come back? It must have been ten minutes since she had gone off to that kitchen, down those miles of passages. His own wife, long dead, would have got that main course into serving dishes before they had sat down to the hors d'oeuvres.

'Get a qualification, that's the thing,' he said. In the distance he heard the wheels of a trolley coming. It was a more welcome sound than that of the wheels of the train one has awaited for an hour on a cold platform. He didn't like the woman, but anything was better than being alone with Hugo. Why not get it over now, he thought, before they began on the amazingly small roasted chicken which had appeared? He managed a smile. He said, 'I can tell you've both fallen on your feet. I'm quite sure, Hugo, you'll look back on all this when you're a successful accountant and thank God you and Frasers parted company.'

And that ought to be that. They had put him through their inquisition and now perhaps they would let him eat this overcooked mess that passed for dinner in peace. At last they would talk of something else, not leave it to him who had been making the running all the evening.

But instead of conversation, there was a deep silence. No one seemed to have anything to say. And although Duncan, working manfully at his chicken wing, racked his brains for a topic, he could think of nothing. Their house, his flat, the workpeople at Frasers, his car, the cost of living, her job, Hugo's course, Christmas past, summer to come, all these subjects must inevitably lead by a direct route back to Hugo's dismissal. And Duncan saw with irritable despair that *all* subjects would lead to it because he was he and they were they, and the dismissal lay between them like an unavoidable spectre at their dismal feast. From time to time he lifted his eyes from his plate, hoping she would respond to that famous smile of his, that smile that was growing stiff with insincere use, but each time he looked at her he saw that she was staring fixedly at him, eating hardly anything, her expression concentrated, dispassionate and somehow dogged. And her eyes had lost their kingfisher flash. They were dull and dead like smoky glass.

So they hadn't had enough then, she and her subdued morose husband? They wanted to see him abject, not merely referring with open frankness to the dismissal as he had done, but explaining it, apologising. Well, they should have his explanation. There was no escape. Carefully, he placed his knife and fork side by side on his empty plate. Precisely, but very politely, he refused his hostess's offer of more. He took a deep breath as he often did at the beginning of a board meeting, as he had so very often done at those board meetings when Hugo Crouch pressed insistently for staff rises.

'My dear Elizabeth,' he began, 'my dear Hugo, I know why you asked me here tonight and what you've been hinting at ever since I arrived. And because I want to enjoy your very delightful company without any more awkwardness, I'm going to do here and now what you very obviously want me to do – that is, explain just how it happened that I suggested Hugo would be happier away from Frasers.'

Elizabeth said, 'Now, Duncan, listen …'

'You can say your piece in a moment, Elizabeth. Perhaps you'll be surprised when I say *I am entirely to blame* for what happened. Yes, I admit it, the fault was mine.' He lifted one hand to silence Hugo. 'No, Hugo, let me finish. As I said, the fault was mine. I made an error of judgement. Oh, yes, I did. I should have been a better judge of men. I should have been able to see when I promoted you that you weren't up to the job. I blame myself for not understanding – well, your limitations.'

They were silent. They didn't look at him or at each other.

'We men in responsible positions,' he said, 'are to blame when the men we appoint can't rise to the heights we envisage for them. We lack vision, that's all. I take the whole burden of it on my shoulders. So shall we forgive and forget?'

He had seldom seen people look so embarrassed, so shame-faced. It just went to show that they were no match for him. His statement had been the last thing they had expected and it was unanswerable. He handed her his plate with its little graveyard of chicken bones among the potato skins, and as she took it he saw a look of baulked fury cross her face.

'Well, Elizabeth,' he said, unable to resist, 'am I forgiven?'

'It's too late now. It's past,' she said in a very cold stony voice. 'It's too late for any of this.'

'I'm sorry if I haven't given you the explanation you wanted, my dear. I've simply told you the truth.'

She didn't say any more. Hugo didn't say anything. And suddenly Duncan felt most uncomfortable. Their condemnatory faces, the way they both seemed to shrink away from him – it was almost too much. His heart began to pound and he had to tell himself that a racing heart meant nothing, that it was pain and not palpitations he must fear. He reached for one of his little white pills ostentatiously, hoping they would notice what they had done to him.

When still they didn't speak, he said, 'I think perhaps I should go now.'

'But you haven't had coffee,' said Elizabeth.

'Just the same, it might be better …'

'Please stay and have coffee,' she said firmly, almost sternly, and then she forced a smile. 'I insist.'

Back in the sitting room they offered him brandy. He refused it because he had to drive home, and the sooner he could begin that drive the happier he would be. Hugo had a large brandy which he drank at a gulp, the way brandy should never be drunk unless one has had a shock or is steeling oneself for something. Elizabeth had picked up the evening paper and was talking in a very artificial way about a murder case which appeared on the front page.

'I really must go,' said Duncan.

'Have some more coffee. It's not ten yet.'

Why did they want him to stay? Or, rather, why did she? Hugo was once more busy with the brandy bottle. Duncan thought his company must be as tiresome to them as theirs was to him. They had got what they wanted, hadn't they? He drank his second cup of coffee so quickly that it scalded his mouth and then he got up.

'I'll get an umbrella. I'll come out with you,' said Hugo.

'Thank you.' It was over. He was going to make his escape

and he need never see them again. And suddenly he felt that he wouldn't be able to get out of that house fast enough. Really, since he had made his little speech, the atmosphere had been thoroughly disagreeable. 'Good night, Elizabeth,' he said. What platitudes could he think of that weren't too ludicrous? 'Thank you for the meal. Perhaps we may meet again someday.'

'I hope we shall and soon, Duncan,' she said, but she didn't give him her cheek. Through the open door the rain was driving in against her long skirt. She stood there, watching him go out with Hugo, letting the light pour out to guide them round the corner of the house.

As soon as he was round that corner, Duncan felt an unpleasant jerk of shock. His car lights were dimly on, headlights on but with the feeble glow of sidelights.

'How did I come to do a thing like that?'

'I suppose you left them on to see your way to the door,' said Hugo, 'and then forgot them.'

'I'm sure I did *not*.'

'You must have. Hold the umbrella and I'll try the ignition.' Leaving Duncan on the flooded path under the inadequate umbrella, Hugo got into the driving seat and inserted the ignition key. The lights gave a flash and went out. Nothing else happened at all. It was now pitch dark. 'Not a spark,' said Hugo. 'Your battery's flat.'

'It *can't* be.'

'I'm afraid it is. Try for yourself.'

Duncan tried, getting very wet in the process.

'We'd better go back in the house. We'll get soaked out here.'

'What's the matter?' said Elizabeth, who was still standing in the doorway.

'His battery's flat. The car won't start.'

Of course it wasn't their fault, but somehow Duncan felt it was. It had happened, after all, at their house to which they had fetched him for a disgraceful purpose. He didn't bother to soften his annoyance.

'I'm afraid I'll just have to borrow your car, Hugo.'

Elizabeth closed the door. 'We don't have a car anymore. We couldn't afford to run it. It was either keeping a car or taking the boys away from school, so we sold it.'

'I see. Then if I might just use your phone, I'll ring for a hire car. I've a mini-cab number in my wallet.' One look at her face told him that wasn't going to be possible either. 'Now you'll say you've had the phone cut off.' Damn her! Damn them both!

'We could have afforded it, of course. We just didn't need it anymore. I'm sorry, Duncan. I just don't know what you can do. But we may as well all go and sit down where it's warmer.'

'I don't want to sit down,' Duncan almost shouted. 'I have to get home.' He shook off the hand she had laid on his arm and which seemed to be forcibly detaining him. 'I must just walk to the nearest house *with* a phone.'

Hugo opened the door. The rain was more like a wall of water than a series of falling drops. 'In this?'

'Then what am I supposed to do?' Duncan cried fretfully.

'Stay the night,' said Elizabeth calmly. 'I really don't know what you can do but stay the night.'

*

The bed was just what he would have expected a bed in the Crouch ménage to be, hard, narrow and cold. She had given him a hot water bottle which was an object he hadn't set eyes on in ten years. And Hugo had lent him a pair of pyjamas. All the time this was going on he had protested that he couldn't stay, that there must be some other way, but in the end he had yielded. Not that they had been welcoming. They had treated the whole thing rather as if – well, how had they treated it? Duncan lay in the dark, clutching the bottle between his knees, and tried to assess just what their attitude had been. Fatalistic, he thought, that was it. They had behaved as if this were inevitable, that there was no escape for him and here, like it or not, he must stay.

Escape was a ridiculous word, of course, but it was the sort of word you used when you were trapped somewhere for a whole night in the home of people who were obviously antagonistic, if not hostile. Why had he been such a fool as to leave those car lights on? He couldn't remember that he had done and yet he must have. Nobody else would have turned them on. Why should they?

He wished they would go to bed too. That they hadn't he could tell by the light, the rectangular outline of dazzlement that showed round the frame of his bedroom door. And he could hear them talking, not the words but the buzz of conversation. These late-Victorian houses were atrociously built, you could hear every sound. The rain drumming on the roof sounded as if it were pounding on cardboard rather than on slates. He didn't think there was much prospect of sleep. How could he sleep with the noise and all that on his mind, the worry of getting the car moved, of finding some way of getting to the office? And it made him feel very uneasy, their staying up like that, particularly as she had said, 'If you'll go into the bathroom first, Duncan, we'll follow you.' Follow him! That must have been all of half an hour ago. He pressed the switch of his bed lamp and saw that it was eleven thirty. Time they were in bed if she had to get to her school in the morning and he to his accountancy course.

Once more in the dark, but for that gold-edged rectangle, he considered the car lights question again. He was certain he had turned them out. Of course it was hard to be certain of anything when you were as upset as he. The pressure they had put on him had been simply horrible, and the worst moments those when he had been alone with Hugo while that woman was fishing out of her oven the ancient pullet she'd dished up to him. Really, she'd been a hell of a time getting that main course when you considered what it had amounted to. Could she ...? Only a madwoman would do such a thing, and what possible motive could she have had? But if you lived in a remote place and you wanted someone to stay in your house overnight, if you wanted to *keep* them there, how better than to immobilise their car? He shivered, even while he told himself such fancies were absurd.

At any rate, they were coming up now. Every board in the house creaked and the stairs played a tune like a broken old violin. He heard Hugo mumble something – the man had drunk far too much brandy – and then she said, 'Leave all the rest to me.'

Another shiver, that hadn't very much to do with the cold, ran through him. He couldn't think why he had shivered. Surely that was quite a natural thing for a woman to say on going to bed? She only meant, You go to bed and I'll lock up and turn off the lights. And yet it was a phrase that was familiar to him in quite another context. Turning on his side away from the light and into fresh caverns of icy sheet, he tried to think where he had heard it. A quotation? Yes – it came from *Macbeth*. Lady Macbeth said it when she and her husband were plotting the old king's murder. And what was the old king's name? Douglas? Donal?

Someone had come out of the bathroom and someone else gone in. Did they always take such ages getting to bed? The lavatory flush roared and a torrent rushed through pipes that seemed to pass under his bed. He heard footsteps cross the landing and a door close. Apparently, they slept in the room next to his. He turned over, longing for the light to go out. It was a pity there was no key in that lock so that he could have locked his door.

As soon as the thought had formed and been uttered in his brain, he thought how fantastic it was. What, lock one's bedroom door in a private house? Suppose his hostess came in the morning with a cup of tea? She would think it very odd. And she might come. She had put this bottle in his bed and had placed a glass of water on the table. Of course he couldn't dream of locking the door, and why should he want to? One of them was in the bathroom *again*.

Suddenly he found himself thinking about one of the men he had sacked and who had threatened him. The man had said, 'Don't think you'll get away with this, and if you show your ugly face within a mile of my place you may not live to regret it.' Of course he had got away with it and had nothing to regret. On the other hand, he hadn't shown himself within a mile of the man's place ... The light had gone out at last. Sleep now, he told himself. Empty your mind or think of something nice. Your summer holiday in the villa, for instance, think about that.

The gardens would be wonderful with the oleanders and the bougainvillea. And the sun would warm his old bones as he sat on his terrace, looking down through the cleft in the pines at the blue triangle of Mediterranean which was brighter and gentler than that woman's eyes ... Never mind the woman, forget her. Perhaps he should have the terrace raised and extended and set up on it that piece of statuary – surely Roman – which he had found in the pinewoods. It would cost a great deal of money, but it was his money. Why shouldn't he spend his own? He must try to be less sensitive, he thought, less troubled by this absurd social conscience which for some reason he had lately developed. Not, he reflected with a faint chuckle, that it actually stopped him spending his money or enjoying himself. It was a nuisance, that was all.

He would have the terrace extended and maybe a black marble floor laid in the *salon*. Fraser's profits looked as if they would hit a new high this year. Why not get that fellow Churchouse to do all their printing for them? If he was really down on his luck and desperate he'd be bound to work for a cut rate, jump at the chance, no doubt ...

God damn it, it was too much! They were talking in there. He could hear their whisperings, rapid, emotional almost, through the wall. They were an absurd couple, no sense of humour between the pair of them. Intense, like characters out of some tragedy.

'The labour we delight in physics pain' – Macbeth had said that, Macbeth who killed the old king. And she had said it to him, Duncan, when he had apologised for the trouble he was causing. The king was called Duncan too. Of course he was. He was called Duncan and so was the old king and he too, in a way, was an old king, the monarch of the Fraser empire. Whisper, whisper, breathed the walls.

He sat up and put on the light. With the light on he felt better. He was sure, though, that he hadn't left those car lights on. 'Leave all the rest to me ...' Why say that? Why not say what everyone said, 'I'll see to everything'? Macbeth and his wife had entertained the old king in their house and murdered him in his bed, although he had done them no harm, done nothing but be king. So it wasn't a parallel, was it? For he, Duncan Fraser, had done something, something which might merit vengeance. He had sacked Hugo Crouch and taken away his livelihood. It wasn't a parallel.

He turned off the light, sighed and lay down again. They were still whispering. He heard the floor creak as one of them came out of the bedroom. It wasn't a parallel – it was worse. Why hadn't he seen that? Lady Macbeth and her husband had no cause, no cause ... A sweat broke out on his face and he reached for the glass of water. But he didn't drink. It was stupid not to but ... The morning would soon come. 'O, never shall sun that morrow see ...!' Where did that come from? Need he ask?

Whoever it was in the bathroom had left it and gone back to the other one. But only for a moment. Again he heard the boards creak, again someone was moving about on that dark landing. Dark, yes, pitch-dark, for they hadn't switched the light on this time. And Duncan felt then the first thrill of real fear, the like of which he hadn't known since he was a little boy and had been shut up in the nursery cupboard of his father's manse. He mustn't be afraid, he mustn't. He must think of his heart. Why should they want vengeance? He'd explained. He'd told them the truth, taking the full burden of blame on himself.

The room was so dark that he didn't see the door handle turn. He heard it. It creaked very softly. His heart began a slow steady pounding and he contracted his body, forcing it back against the wall. Whoever it was had come into the room. He could see the shape of him – or her – as a denser blackness in the dark.

'What …? Who …?' he said, quavering, his throat dry.

The shape grew fluid, glided away, and the door closed softly. They wanted to see if he was asleep. They would kill him when he was asleep. He sat up, switched on the light and put his face in his hands. 'O, never shall sun that morrow see!' He'd put all that furniture against the door, that chest of drawers, his bed, the chair. His throat was parched now and he reached for the water, taking a long draught. It was icy cold.

They weren't whispering anymore. They were waiting in silence. He got up and put his coat round him. In the bitter cold he began lugging the furniture away from the walls, lifting the iron bedstead that felt so small and narrow when he was in it but was so hideously weighty.

Straightening up from his second attempt, he felt it, the pain in his chest and down his left arm. It came like a clamp, a clamp being screwed and at the same time slowly heated red-hot. It took his body in hot iron fingers and squeezed his ribs. And sweat began to pour from him as if the temperature in the room had suddenly risen tremendously. O God, O God, the water in the glass! They would have to get him a doctor, they would have to, they couldn't be so pitiless. He was old and tired and his heart was bad.

He pulled the coat round the pain and staggered out into the black passage. Their door – where was their door? He found it by fumbling at the walls, scrabbling like an imprisoned animal, and when he found it he kicked it open and swayed on the threshold, holding the pain in both his hands.

They were sitting on their bed with their backs to him, not in bed but sitting there, the shapes of them silhouetted against the light of a small low-bulbed bed lamp.

'Oh, please,' he said, 'please help me. Don't kill me, I beg you not to kill me. I'll go on my knees to you. I know I've done wrong, I did a terrible thing. I didn't make an error of judgement. I sacked Hugo because he wanted too much for the staff, he wanted more money for everyone and I couldn't let them have it. I wanted my new car and my holidays. I had to have my villa – so beautiful, my villa and my gardens. Ah, God, I know I was greedy, but I've borne the guilt of it for months, every day on my conscience, the guilt of it ...' They turned two white faces, implacable, merciless. They rose and came scrambling across their bed. 'Have pity on me,' he screamed. 'Don't kill me. I'll give you everything I've got, I'll give you a million ...'

But they had seized him with their hands and it was too late. She had told him it was too late.

*

'In our house!' she said.

'Don't,' said Hugo. 'That's what Lady Macbeth said. What does it matter whether it was in our house or not?'

'I wish I'd never invited him.'

'Well, it was your idea. You said let's have him here because he's a widower and lonely. I didn't want him. It was ghastly the way he insisted on talking about firing me when we wanted to keep off the subject at any price. I was utterly fed up when he had to stay the night.'

'What do we do now?' said Elizabeth.

'Get the police, I should think, or a doctor. It's stopped raining. I'll get dressed and go.'

'But you're not well! You kept throwing up.'

'I'm OK now. I drank too much brandy. It was such a strain, all of it, nobody knowing what to talk about. God, what a business! He was all right when you went into his room just now, wasn't he?'

'Half-asleep. I thought. I was going to apologise for all the racket you were making but he seemed nearly asleep. Did you get any of what he was trying to say when he came in here? I didn't.'

'No, it was just gibberish. We couldn't have done anything for him, darling. We did try to catch him before he fell.'

'I know.'

'He had a bad heart.'

'In more ways than one, poor old man,' said Elizabeth, and she laid a blanket gently over Duncan, though he was past feeling heat or cold or guilt or fear or anything anymore.

The Gardener

E. F. Benson

Two friends of mine, Hugh Grainger and his wife, had taken for a month of Christmas holiday the house in which we were to witness such strange manifestations, and when I received an invitation from them to spend a fortnight there I returned them an enthusiastic affirmative. Well already did I know that pleasant heathery countryside, and most intimate was my acquaintance with the subtle hazards of its most charming golf links. Golf, I was given to understand, was to occupy the solid day for Hugh and me, so that Margaret should never be obliged to set her hand to the implements with which the game, so detestable to her, was conducted ...

I arrived there while yet the daylight lingered, and as my hosts were out, I took a ramble round the place. The house and garden stood on a plateau facing south; below it were a couple of acres of pasture that sloped down to a vagrant stream crossed by a footbridge, by the side of which stood a thatched cottage with a vegetable patch surrounding it. A path ran close past this across the pasture from a wicket gate in the garden, conducted you over the footbridge, and, so my remembered sense of geography told me, must constitute a shortcut to the links that lay not half a mile beyond. The cottage itself was clearly on the land of the little estate, and I at once supposed it to be the gardener's house. What went against so obvious and simple a theory was that it appeared to be untenanted. No wreath of smoke, though the evening was chilly, curled from its chimneys, and, coming closer, I fancied it had that air of 'waiting' about it which we so often conjure into unused habitations. There it stood, with no sign of life whatever about it, though ready, as its apparently perfect state of repair seemed to warrant, for fresh tenants to put the breath of life into it again. Its little garden, too, though the palings were neat and newly painted, told the same tale; the beds were untended and unweeded, and in the flower-border by the front door was a row of chrysanthemums, which had withered on their stems. But all this was but the impression of a moment, and I did not pause as I passed it, but crossed the footbridge and went on up the heathery slope that lay beyond. My geography was not at fault, for presently I saw the clubhouse just in front of me. Hugh no doubt would be just about coming in from his afternoon round, and so we would walk back together. On reaching the clubhouse, however, the steward told me that not five minutes before Mrs Grainger had called in her car for her husband, and I therefore retraced my steps by the path along which I had already come. But I made a detour, as a golfer will, to walk up the fairway of the seventeenth and eighteenth holes just for the pleasure of recognition, and looked respectfully at the yawning sandpit which so inexorably guards the eighteenth green, wondering in what circumstances I should visit it next, whether with a step complacent and superior, knowing that my ball reposed safely on the green beyond, or with the heavy footfall of one who knows that laborious delving lies before him.

The light of the winter evening had faded fast, and when I crossed the footbridge on my return the dusk had gathered. To my right, just beside the path, lay the cottage, the whitewashed walls of which gleamed whitely in the gloaming; and as I turned my glance back from it to the rather narrow plank which bridged the stream I thought I caught out of the tail of my eye some light from one of its windows, which thus disproved my theory that it was untenanted. But when I looked directly at it again I saw that I was mistaken: some reflection in the glass of the red lines of sunset in the west must have deceived me, for in the inclement twilight it looked more desolate than ever. Yet I lingered by the wicket gate in its low palings, for though all exterior evidence bore witness to its emptiness, some inexplicable feeling assured me, quite irrationally, that this was not so, and that there was somebody there. Certainly there was nobody visible, but, so this absurd idea informed me, he might be at the back of the cottage concealed from me by the intervening structure, and, still oddly, still unreasonably, it became a matter of importance to my mind to ascertain whether this was so or not, so clearly had my perceptions told me that the place was empty, and so firmly had some conviction assured me that it was tenanted. To cover my inquisitiveness, in case there was someone there, I could inquire whether this path was a short-cut to the house at which I was staying, and, rather rebelling at what I was doing, I went through the small garden, and rapped at the door. There was no answer, and, after waiting for a response to a second summons, and having tried the door and found it locked, I made the circuit of the house. Of course there was no one there, and I told myself that I was just like a man who looks under his bed for a burglar and would be beyond measure astonished if he found one.

My hosts were at the house when I arrived, and we spent a cheerful two hours before dinner in such desultory and eager conversation as is proper between friends who have not met for some time. Between Hugh Grainger and his wife it is always impossible to light on a subject which does not vividly interest one or other of them, and golf, politics, the needs of Russia, cooking, ghosts, the possible victory over Mount Everest, and the income tax were among the topics which we passionately discussed. With all these plates spinning, it was easy to whip up any one of them, and the subject of spooks generally was lighted upon again and again.

'Margaret is on the high road to madness,' remarked Hugh on one of these occasions, 'for she has begun using planchette. If you use planchette for six months, I am told, most careful doctors will conscientiously certify you as insane. She's got five months more before she goes to Bedlam.'

'Does it work?' I asked.

'Yes, it says most interesting things,' said Margaret. 'It says things that never entered my head. We'll try it tonight.'

'Oh, not tonight,' said Hugh. 'Let's have an evening off.'

Margaret disregarded this.

'It's no use asking planchette questions,' she went on, 'because there is in your mind some sort of answer to them. If I ask whether it will be fine tomorrow, for instance, it is probably I – though indeed I don't mean to push – who makes the pencil say "yes".'

'And then it usually rains,' remarked Hugh.

'Not always: don't interrupt. The interesting thing is to let the pencil write what it chooses. Very often it only makes loops and curves – though they may mean something – and every now and then a word comes, of the significance of which I have no idea whatever, so I clearly couldn't have suggested it. Yesterday evening, for instance, it wrote "gardener" over and over again. Now what did that mean? The gardener here is a Methodist with a chin-beard. Could it have meant him? Oh, it's time to dress. Please don't be late, my cook is so sensitive about soup.'

We rose, and some connection of ideas about 'gardener' linked itself up in my mind.

'By the way, what's that cottage in the field by the footbridge?' I asked. 'Is that the gardener's cottage?'

'It used to be,' said Hugh. 'But the chin-beard doesn't live there: in fact nobody lives there. It's empty. If I was owner here, I should put the chin-beard into it, and take the rent off his wages. Some people have no idea of economy. Why did you ask?'

I saw Margaret was looking at me rather attentively.

'Curiosity,' I said. 'Idle curiosity.'

'I don't believe it was,' said she.

'But it was,' I said. 'It was idle curiosity to know whether the house was inhabited. As I passed it, going down to the clubhouse, I felt sure it was empty, but coming back I felt so sure that there was someone there that I rapped at the door, and indeed walked round it.'

Hugh had preceded us upstairs, as she lingered a little.

'And there was no one there?' she asked. 'It's odd: I had just the same feeling as you about it.'

'That explains planchette writing "gardener" over and over again,' said I. 'You had the gardener's cottage on your mind.'

'How ingenious!' said Margaret. 'Hurry up and dress.'

A gleam of strong moonlight between my drawn curtains when I went up to bed that night led me to look out. My room faced the garden and the fields which I had traversed that afternoon, and all was vividly illuminated by the full moon. The thatched cottage with its white walls close by the stream was very distinct, and once more, I suppose, the reflection of the light on the glass of one of its windows made it appear that the room was lit within. It struck me as odd that twice that day this illusion should have been presented to me, but now a yet odder thing happened. Even as I looked the light was extinguished.

The morning did not at all bear out the fine promise of the clear night, for when I woke the wind was squealing, and sheets of rain from the south-west were dashed against my panes. Golf was wholly out of the question, and, though the violence of the storm abated a little in the afternoon, the rain dripped with a steady sullenness. But I wearied of indoors, and, since the two others entirely refused to set foot outside, I went forth mackintoshed to get a breath of air. By way of an object in my tramp, I took the road to the links in preference

to the muddy shortcut through the fields, with the intention
of engaging a couple of caddies for Hugh and myself next
morning, and lingered awhile over illustrated papers in the
smoking room. I must have read for longer than I knew,
for a sudden beam of sunset light suddenly illuminated my
page, and looking up, I saw that the rain had ceased, and that
evening was fast coming on. So instead of taking the long
detour by the road again, I set forth homewards by the path
across the fields. That gleam of sunset was the last of the day,
and once again, just as twenty-four hours ago, I crossed the
footbridge in the gloaming. Till that moment, as far as I was
aware, I had not thought at all about the cottage there, but
now in a flash the light I had seen there last night, suddenly
extinguished, recalled itself to my mind, and at the same
moment I felt that invincible conviction that the cottage was
tenanted. Simultaneously in these swift processes of thought
I looked towards it, and saw standing by the door the figure
of a man. In the dusk I could distinguish nothing of his face,
if indeed it was turned to me, and only got the impression
of a tallish fellow, thickly built. He opened the door, from
which there came a dim light as of a lamp, entered, and shut
it after him.

So then my conviction was right. Yet I had been distinctly told that the cottage was empty: who, then, was he
that entered as if returning home? Once more, this time
with a certain qualm of fear, I rapped on the door, intend-
ing to put some trivial question; and rapped again, this time
more drastically, so that there could be no question that my
summons was unheard. But still I got no reply, and finally
I tried the handle of the door. It was locked. Then, with

difficulty mastering an increasing terror, I made the circuit of the cottage, peering into each unshuttered window. All was dark within, though but two minutes ago I had seen the gleam of light escape from the opened door.

Just because some chain of conjecture was beginning to form itself in my mind, I made no allusion to this odd adventure, and after dinner Margaret, amid protests from Hugh, got out the planchette which had persisted in writing 'gardener'. My surmise was, of course, utterly fantastic, but I wanted to convey no suggestion of any sort to Margaret … For a long time the pencil skated over her paper making loops and curves and peaks like a temperature chart, and she had begun to yawn and weary over her experiment before any coherent word emerged. And then, in the oddest way, her head nodded forward and she seemed to have fallen asleep.

Hugh looked up from his book and spoke in a whisper to me.

'She fell asleep the other night over it,' he said.

Margaret's eyes were closed, and she breathed the long, quiet breaths of slumber, and then her hand began to move with a curious firmness. Right across the big sheet of paper went a level line of writing, and at the end her hand stopped with a jerk, and she woke.

She looked at the paper.

'Hullo,' she said. 'Ah, one of you has been playing a trick on me!'

We assured her that this was not so, and she read what she had written.

'Gardener, gardener,' it ran. 'I am the gardener. I want to come in. I can't find her here.'

'O Lord, that gardener again!' said Hugh.

Looking up from the paper, I saw Margaret's eyes fixed on mine, and even before she spoke I knew what her thought was.

'Did you come home by the empty cottage?' she asked.

'Yes: why?'

'Still empty?' she said in a low voice. 'Or – or anything else?'

I did not want to tell her just what I had seen – or what, at any rate, I thought I had seen. If there was going to be anything odd, anything worth observation, it was far better that our respective impressions should not fortify each other.

'I tapped again, and there was no answer,' I said.

Presently there was a move to bed: Margaret initiated it, and after she had gone upstairs Hugh and I went to the front door to interrogate the weather. Once more the moon shone in a clear sky, and we strolled out along the flagged path that fronted the house. Suddenly Hugh turned quickly and pointed to the angle of the house.

'Who on earth is that?' he said. 'Look! There! He has gone round the corner.'

I had but the glimpse of a tallish man of heavy build.

'Didn't you see him?' asked Hugh. 'I'll just go round the house, and find him; I don't want anyone prowling round us at night. Wait here, will you, and if he comes round the other corner ask him what his business is.'

Hugh had left me, in our stroll, close by the front door which was open, and there I waited until he should have made his circuit. He had hardly disappeared when I heard, quite distinctly, a rather quick but heavy footfall coming along the paved walk towards me from the opposite direction. But there was absolutely no one to be seen who made this sound of rapid walking. Closer and closer to me came the steps of the invisible one, and then with a shudder of horror I felt somebody unseen push by me as I stood on the threshold. That shudder was not merely of the spirit, for the touch of him was that of ice on my hand. I tried to seize this impalpable intruder, but he slipped from me, and next moment I heard his steps on the parquet of the floor inside. Some door within opened and shut, and I heard no more of him. Next moment Hugh came running round the corner of the house from which the sound of steps had approached.

'But where is he?' he asked. 'He was not twenty yards in front of me – a big, tall fellow.'

'I saw nobody,' I said. 'I heard his step along the walk, but there was nothing to be seen.'

'And then?' asked Hugh.

'Whatever it was seemed to brush by me, and go into the house,' said I.

There had certainly been no sound of steps on the bare oak stairs, and we searched room after room through the ground floor of the house. The dining-room door and that of the smoking room were locked, that into the drawing room was open, and the only other door which could have furnished the impression of an opening and a shutting was that into the kitchen and servants' quarters. Here again our quest was fruitless; through pantry and scullery and boot room and servants' hall we searched, but all was empty and quiet. Finally we came to the kitchen, which too was empty. But by the fire there was set a rocking chair, and this was oscillating to and fro as if someone, lately sitting there, had just quitted it. There it stood gently rocking, and this seemed to convey the sense of a presence, invisible now, more than even the sight of him who surely had been sitting there could have done. I remember wanting to steady it and stop it, and yet my hand refused to go forth to it.

What we had seen, and in especial what we had not seen, would have been sufficient to furnish most people with a broken night, and assuredly I was not among the strong-minded exceptions. Long I lay wide-eyed and open-eared, and when at last I dozed I was plucked from the border-land of sleep by the sound, muffled but unmistakable, of someone moving about the house. It occurred to me that the steps might be those of Hugh conducting a lonely exploration, but even while I wondered a tap came at the door of communication between our rooms, and, in answer to my response, it appeared that he had come to see whether it was I thus uneasily wandering. Even as we spoke the step passed my door, and the stairs leading to the floor above creaked to its ascent. Next moment it sounded directly above our heads in some attics in the roof.

'Those are not the servants' bedrooms,' said Hugh. 'No one sleeps there. Let us look once more: it must be somebody.'

With lit candles we made our stealthy way upstairs, and just when we were at the top of the flight, Hugh, a step ahead of me, uttered a sharp exclamation.

'But something is passing by me!' he said, and he clutched at the empty air. Even as he spoke, I experienced the same sensation, and the moment afterwards the stairs below us creaked again, as the unseen passed down.

All night long that sound of steps moved about the passages, as if someone was searching the house, and as I lay and listened that message which had come through the pencil of the planchette to Margaret's fingers occurred to me. 'I want to come in. I cannot find her here.' ... Indeed someone had come in, and was sedulous in his search. He was the gardener, it would seem. But what gardener was this invisible seeker, and for whom did he seek?

Even as when some bodily pain ceases it is difficult to recall with any vividness what the pain was like, so next morning, as I dressed, I found myself vainly trying to recapture the horror of the spirit which had accompanied these nocturnal adventures. I remembered that something within me had sickened as I watched the movements of the rocking chair the night before and as I heard the steps along the paved way outside, and by that invisible pressure against me knew that someone had entered the house. But now in the sane and tranquil morning, and all day under the serene winter sun, I could not realise what it had been. The presence, like the bodily pain, had to be there for the realisation of it, and all day it was absent. Hugh felt the same; he was even disposed to be humorous on the subject.

'Well, he's had a good look,' he said, 'whoever he is, and whomever he was looking for. By the way, not a word to Margaret, please. She heard nothing of these perambulations, nor of the entry of – of whatever it was. Not gardener, anyhow: who ever heard of a gardener spending his time walking about the house? If there were steps all over the potato patch, I might have been with you.'

Margaret had arranged to drive over to have tea with

some friends of hers that afternoon, and in consequence Hugh and I refreshed ourselves at the clubhouse after our game, and it was already dusk when for the third day in succession I passed homewards by the whitewashed cottage. But tonight I had no sense of it being subtly occupied; it stood mournfully desolate, as is the way of untenanted houses, and no light nor semblance of such gleamed from its windows. Hugh, to whom I had told the odd impressions I had received there, gave them a reception as flippant as that which he had accorded to the memories of the night, and he was still being humorous about them when we came to the door of the house.

'A psychic disturbance, old boy,' he said. 'Like a cold in the head. Hullo, the door's locked.'

He rang and rapped, and from inside came the noise of a turned key and withdrawn bolts.

'What's the door locked for?' he asked his servant who opened it.

The man shifted from one foot to the other.

'The bell rang half an hour ago, sir,' he said, 'and when I came to answer it there was a man standing outside, and—'

'Well?' asked Hugh.

'I didn't like the looks of him, sir,' he said, 'and I asked him his business. He didn't say anything, and then he must have gone pretty smartly away, for I never saw him go.'

'Where did he seem to go?' asked Hugh, glancing at me.

'I can't rightly say, sir. He didn't seem to go at all. Something seemed to brush by me.'

'That'll do,' said Hugh rather sharply.

*

Margaret had not come in from her visit, but when soon after the crunch of the motor wheels was heard Hugh reiterated his wish that nothing should be said to her about the impression which now, apparently, a third person shared with us. She came in with a flush of excitement on her face.

'Never laugh at my planchette again,' she said. 'I've heard the most extraordinary story from Maud Ashfield – horrible, but so frightfully interesting.'

'Out with it,' said Hugh.

'Well, there was a gardener here,' she said. 'He used to live at that little cottage by the foot bridge, and when the family were up in London he and his wife used to be caretakers and live here.'

Hugh's glance and mine met: then he turned away. I knew, as certainly as if I was in his mind, that his thoughts were identical with my own.

'He married a wife much younger than himself,' continued Margaret, 'and gradually he became frightfully jealous of her. And one day in a fit of passion he strangled her with his own hands. A little while after someone came to the cottage, and found him sobbing over her, trying to restore her. They went for the police, but before they came he had cut his own throat. Isn't it all horrible? But surely it's rather curious that the planchette said "Gardener. I am the gardener. I want to come in. I can't find her here." You see I knew nothing about it. I shall do planchette again tonight. Oh dear me, the post goes in half an hour, and I have a whole budget to send. But respect my planchette for the future, Hughie.'

We talked the situation out when she had gone, but Hugh, unwillingly convinced and yet unwilling to admit that something more than coincidence lay behind that 'planchette nonsense', still insisted that Margaret should be told nothing of what we had heard and seen in the house last night, and of the strange visitor who again this evening, so we must conclude, had made his entry.

'She'll be frightened,' he said, 'and she'll begin imagining things. As for the planchette, as likely as not it will do nothing but scribble and make loops. What's that? Yes: come in!'

There had come from somewhere in the room one sharp, peremptory rap. I did not think it came from the door, but Hugh, when no response replied to his words of admittance, jumped up and opened it. He took a few steps into the hall outside, and returned.

'Didn't you hear it?' he asked.

'Certainly. No one there?'

'Not a soul.'

Hugh came back to the fireplace and rather irritably threw a cigarette which he had just lit into the fender.

'That was rather a nasty jar,' he observed; 'and if you ask me whether I feel comfortable, I can tell you I never felt less comfortable in my life. I'm frightened, if you want to know, and I believe you are too.'

I hadn't the smallest intention of denying this, and he went on.

'We've got to keep a hand on ourselves,' he said. 'There's nothing so infectious as fear, and Margaret mustn't catch it from us. But there's something more than our fear, you know. Something has got into the house and we're up against it. I never believed in such things before. Let's face it for a minute. *What* is it anyhow?'

'If you want to know what I think it is,' said I, 'I believe it to be the spirit of the man who strangled his wife and then cut his throat. But I don't see how it can hurt us. We're afraid of our own fear really.'

'But we're up against it,' said Hugh. 'And what will it do? Good Lord, if I only knew what it would do I shouldn't mind. It's the not knowing ... Well, it's time to dress.'

Margaret was in her highest spirits at dinner. Knowing nothing of the manifestations of that presence which had taken place in the last twenty-four hours, she thought it absorbingly interesting that her planchette should have 'guessed' (so ran her phrase) about the gardener, and from that topic she flitted to an equally interesting form of patience for three which her friend had showed her, promising to initiate us into it after dinner. This she did, and, not knowing that we both above all things wanted to keep planchette at a distance, she was delighted with the success of her game. But suddenly she observed that the evening was burning rapidly away, and swept the cards together at the conclusion of a hand.

'Now just half an hour of planchette,' she said.

'Oh, mayn't we play one more hand?' asked Hugh. 'It's the best game I've seen for years. Planchette will be dismally slow after this.'

'Darling, if the gardener will only communicate again, it won't be slow,' said she.

'But it is such drivel,' said Hugh.

'How rude you are! Read your book, then.'

Margaret had already got out her machine and a sheet of paper, when Hugh rose.

'Please don't do it tonight, Margaret,' he said.

'But why? You needn't attend.'

'Well, I ask you not to, anyhow,' said he.

Margaret looked at him closely.

'Hughie, you've got something on your mind,' she said. 'Out with it. I believe you're nervous. You think there is something queer about. What is it?'

I could see Hugh hesitating as to whether to tell her or not, and I gathered that he chose the chance of her planchette inanely scribbling.

'Go on, then,' he said.

Margaret hesitated: she clearly did not want to vex Hugh, but his insistence must have seemed to her most unreasonable.

'Well, just ten minutes,' she said, 'and I promise not to think of gardeners.'

She had hardly laid her hand on the board when her head fell forward, and the machine began moving. I was sitting close to her, and as it rolled steadily along the paper the writing became visible.

'I have come in,' it ran, 'but still I can't find her. Are you hiding her? I will search the room where you are.'

What else was written but still concealed underneath the planchette I did not know, for at that moment a current of icy air swept round the room, and at the door, this time unmistakably, came a loud, peremptory knock. Hugh sprang to his feet.

'Margaret, wake up,' he said, 'something is coming!'

The door opened, and there moved in the figure of a man. He stood just within the door, his head bent forward, and he turned it from side to side, peering, it would seem, with eyes staring and infinitely sad, into every corner of the room.

'Margaret, Margaret,' cried Hugh again.

But Margaret's eyes were open too; they were fixed on this dreadful visitor.

'Be quiet, Hughie,' she said below her breath, rising as she spoke. The ghost was now looking directly at her. Once the lips above the thick, rust-coloured beard moved, but no sound came forth, the mouth only moved and slavered. He raised his head, and, horror upon horror, I saw that one side of his neck was laid open in a red, glistening gash ...

For how long that pause continued, when we all three stood stiff and frozen in some deadly inhibition to move or speak, I have no idea: I suppose that at the utmost it was a dozen seconds. Then the spectre turned, and went out as it had come. We heard his steps pass along the parqueted floor; there was the sound of bolts withdrawn from the front door, and with a crash that shook the house it slammed to.

'It's all over,' said Margaret. 'God have mercy on him!'

Now the reader may put precisely what construction he pleases on this visitation from the dead. He need not, indeed, consider it to have been a visitation from the dead at all, but say that there had been impressed on the scene, where this murder and suicide happened, some sort of emotional record, which in certain circumstances could translate itself into images visible and invisible. Waves of ether, or what not, may conceivably retain the impress of such scenes; they may be held, so to speak, in solution, ready to be precipitated. Or he may hold that the spirit of the dead man indeed made itself manifest, revisiting in some sort of spiritual penance and remorse the place where his crime was committed. Naturally, no materialist will entertain such an explanation for an instant, but then there is no one so obstinately unreasonable as the materialist. Beyond doubt a dreadful deed was done there, and Margaret's last utterance is not inapplicable.

The Case of Lady Sannox

Arthur Conan Doyle

The relations between Douglas Stone and the notorious Lady
Sannox were very well known both among the fashionable
circles of which she was a brilliant member, and the scientific
bodies which numbered him among their most illustrious
confrères. There was naturally, therefore, a very wide-
spread interest when it was announced one morning that the
lady had absolutely and for ever taken the veil, and that the
world would see her no more. When, at the very tail of this
rumour, there came the assurance that the celebrated operat-
ing surgeon, the man of steel nerves, had been found in the
morning by his valet, seated on one side of his bed, smiling
pleasantly upon the universe, with both legs jammed into one
side of his breeches and his great brain about as valuable as
a cap full of porridge, the matter was strong enough to give
quite a little thrill of interest to folk who had never hoped that
their jaded nerves were capable of such a sensation.

Douglas Stone in his prime was one of the most remarkable men in England. Indeed, he could hardly be said to have ever reached his prime, for he was but nine-and-thirty at the time of this little incident. Those who knew him best were aware that famous as he was as a surgeon, he might have succeeded with even greater rapidity in any of a dozen lines of life. He could have cut his way to fame as a soldier, struggled to it as an explorer, bullied for it in the courts, or built it out of stone and iron as an engineer. He was born to be great, for he could plan what another man dare not do, and he could do what another man dare not plan. In surgery none could follow him. His nerve, his judgement, his intuition, were things apart. Again and again his knife cut away death, but grazed the very springs of life in doing it, until his assistants were as white as the patient. His energy, his audacity, his full-blooded self-confidence – does not the memory of them still linger to the south of Marylebone Road and the north of Oxford Street?

His vices were as magnificent as his virtues, and infinitely more picturesque. Large as was his income, and it was the third largest of all professional men in London, it was far beneath the luxury of his living. Deep in his complex nature lay a rich vein of sensualism, at the sport of which he placed all the prizes of his life. The eye, the ear, the touch, the palate, all were his masters. The bouquet of old vintages, the scent of rare exotics, the curves and tints of the daintiest potteries of Europe, it was to these that the quick-running stream of gold was transformed. And then there came his sudden mad passion for Lady Sannox, when a single interview with two challenging glances and a whispered word set him ablaze.

She was the loveliest woman in London and the only one to him. He was one of the handsomest men in London, but not the only one to her. She had a liking for new experiences, and was gracious to most men who wooed her. It may have been cause or it may have been effect that Lord Sannox looked fifty, though he was but six-and-thirty.

He was a quiet, silent, neutral-tinted man, this lord, with thin lips and heavy eyelids, much given to gardening, and full of home-like habits. He had at one time been fond of acting, had even rented a theatre in London, and on its boards had first seen Miss Marion Dawson, to whom he had offered his hand, his title, and the third of a county. Since his marriage his early hobby had become distasteful to him. Even in private theatricals it was no longer possible to persuade him to exercise the talent which he had often showed that he possessed. He was happier with a spud and a watering can among his orchids and chrysanthemums.

It was quite an interesting problem whether he was absolutely devoid of sense, or miserably wanting in spirit. Did he know his lady's ways and condone them, or was he a mere blind, doting fool? It was a point to be discussed over the teacups in snug little drawing rooms, or with the aid of a cigar in the bow windows of clubs. Bitter and plain were the comments among men upon his conduct. There was but one who had a good word to say for him, and he was the most silent member in the smoking room. He had seen him break in a horse at the University, and it seemed to have left an impression upon his mind.

But when Douglas Stone became the favourite all doubts as to Lord Sannox's knowledge or ignorance were set for ever at rest. There was no subterfuge about Stone. In his high-handed, impetuous fashion, he set all caution and discretion at defiance. The scandal became notorious. A learned body intimated that his name had been struck from the list of its vice-presidents. Two friends implored him to consider his professional credit. He cursed them all three, and spent forty guineas on a bangle to take with him to the lady. He was at her house every evening, and she drove in his carriage in the afternoons. There was not an attempt on either side to conceal their relations; but there came at last a little incident to interrupt them.

It was a dismal winter's night, very cold and gusty, with the wind whooping in the chimneys and blustering against the windowpanes. A thin spatter of rain tinkled on the glass with each fresh sough of the gale, drowning for the instant the dull gurgle and drip from the eaves. Douglas Stone had finished his dinner, and sat by his fire in the study, a glass of rich port upon the malachite table at his elbow. As he raised it to his lips, he held it up against the lamplight, and watched with the eye of a connoisseur the tiny scales of beeswing which floated in its rich ruby depths. The fire, as it spurted up, threw fitful lights upon his bald, clear-cut face, with its widely opened grey eyes, its thick and yet firm lips, and the deep, square jaw, which had something Roman in its strength and its animalism. He smiled from time to time as he nestled back in his luxurious chair. Indeed, he had a right to feel well pleased, for, against the advice of six colleagues, he had performed an operation that day of which only two cases were on record, and the result had been brilliant beyond all expectation. No other man in London would have had the daring to plan, or the skill to execute, such a heroic measure.

But he had promised Lady Sannox to see her that evening and it was already half-past eight. His hand was outstretched to the bell to order the carriage when he heard the dull thud of the knocker. An instant later there was the shuffling of feet in the hall, and the sharp closing of a door.

'A patient to see you, sir, in the consulting room,' said the butler.

'About himself?'

'No, sir; I think he wants you to go out.'

'It is too late,' cried Douglas Stone peevishly. 'I won't go.'

'This is his card, sir.'

The butler presented it upon the gold salver which had been given to his master by the wife of a Prime Minister.

'"Hamil Ali, Smyrna." Hum! The fellow is a Turk, I suppose.'

'Yes, sir. He seems as if he came from abroad, sir. And he's in a terrible way.'

'Tut, tut! I have an engagement. I must go somewhere else. But I'll see him. Show him in here, Pim.'

A few moments later the butler swung open the door and ushered in a small and decrepit man, who walked with a bent back and with the forward push of the face and blink of the eyes which goes with extreme short sight. His face was swarthy, and his hair and beard of the deepest black. In one hand he held a turban of white muslin striped with red, in the other a small chamois-leather bag.

'Good evening,' said Douglas Stone, when the butler had closed the door. 'You speak English, I presume?'

'Yes, sir. I am from Asia Minor, but I speak English when I speak slow.'

'You wanted me to go out, I understand?'

'Yes, sir. I wanted very much that you should see my wife.'

'I could come in the morning, but I have an engagement which prevents me from seeing your wife tonight.'

The Turk's answer was a singular one. He pulled the string which closed the mouth of the chamois-leather bag, and poured a flood of gold onto the table.

'There are one hundred pounds there,' said he, 'and I promise you that it will not take you an hour. I have a cab ready at the door.'

Douglas Stone glanced at his watch. An hour would not make it too late to visit Lady Sannox. He had been there later. And the fee was an extraordinarily high one. He had been pressed by his creditors lately, and he could not afford to let such a chance pass. He would go.

'What is the case?' he asked.

'Oh, it is so sad a one! So sad a one! You have not, perhaps heard of the daggers of the Almohades?'

'Never.'

'Ah, they are Eastern daggers of a great age and of a singular shape, with the hilt like what you call a stirrup. I am a curiosity dealer, you understand, and that is why I have come to England from Smyrna, but next week I go back once more. Many things I brought with me, and I have a few things left, but among them, to my sorrow, is one of these daggers.'

'You will remember that I have an appointment, sir,' said the surgeon, with some irritation; 'pray confine yourself to the necessary details.'

'You will see that it is necessary. Today my wife fell down in a faint in the room in which I keep my wares, and she cut her lower lip upon this cursed dagger of Almohades.'

'I see,' said Douglas Stone, rising. 'And you wish me to dress the wound?'

'No, no, it is worse than that.'

'What then?'

'These daggers are poisoned.'

'Poisoned!'

'Yes, and there is no man, East or West, who can tell now what is the poison or what the cure. But all that is known I know, for my father was in this trade before me, and we have had much to do with these poisoned weapons.'

'What are the symptoms?'

'Deep sleep, and death in thirty hours.'

'And you say there is no cure. Why then should you pay me this considerable fee?'

'No drug can cure, but the knife may.'

'And how?'

'The poison is slow of absorption. It remains for hours in the wound.'

'Washing, then, might cleanse it?'

'No more than in a snake bite. It is too subtle and too deadly.'

'Excision of the wound, then?'

'That is it. If it be on the finger, take the finger off. So said my father always. But think of where this wound is, and that it is my wife. It is dreadful!'

But familiarity with such grim matters may take the finer edge from a man's sympathy. To Douglas Stone this was

75

already an interesting case, and he brushed aside as irrelevant the feeble objections of the husband.

'It appears to be that or nothing,' said he brusquely. 'It is better to lose a lip than a life.'

'Ah, yes, I know that you are right. Well, well, it is kismet, and it must be faced. I have the cab, and you will come with me and do this thing.'

Douglas Stone took his case of bistouries from a drawer, and placed it with a roll of bandage and a compress of lint in his pocket. He must waste no more time if he were to see Lady Sannox.

'I am ready,' said he, pulling on his overcoat. 'Will you take a glass of wine before you go out into this cold air?'

His visitor shrank away, with a protesting hand upraised.

'You forget that I am a Mussulman, and a true follower of the Prophet,' said he. 'But tell me what is the bottle of green glass which you have placed in your pocket?'

'It is chloroform.'

'Ah, that also is forbidden to us. It is a spirit, and we make no use of such things.'

'What! You would allow your wife to go through an operation without an anaesthetic?'

'Ah! She will feel nothing, poor soul. The deep sleep has already come on, which is the first working of the poison. And then I have given her of our Smyrna opium. Come, sir, for already an hour has passed.'

As they stepped out into the darkness, a sheet of rain was driven in upon their faces, and the hall lamp, which dangled from the arm of a marble Caryatid, went out with a fluff. Pim, the butler, pushed the heavy door to, straining hard with his shoulder against the wind, while the two men groped their way towards the yellow glare which showed where the cab was waiting. An instant later they were rattling upon their journey.

'Is it far?' asked Douglas Stone.

'Oh, no. We have a very little quiet place off the Euston Road.'

The surgeon pressed the spring of his repeater and listened to the little tings which told him the hour. It was a quarter past nine. He calculated the distances, and the short time which it would take him to perform so trivial an operation. He ought to reach Lady Sannox by ten o'clock. Through the fogged windows he saw the blurred gas lamps dancing past, with occasionally the broader glare of a shop front. The rain was pelting and rattling upon the leathern top of the carriage, and the wheels swashed as they rolled through puddle and mud. Opposite to him the white headgear of his companion gleamed faintly through the obscurity. The surgeon felt in his pockets and arranged his needles, his ligatures and his safety pins, that no time might be wasted when they arrived. He chafed with impatience and drummed his foot upon the floor.

But the cab slowed down at last and pulled up. In an instant Douglas Stone was out, and the Smyrna merchant's toe was at his very heel.

'You can wait,' said he to the driver.

It was a mean-looking house in a narrow and sordid street. The surgeon, who knew his London well, cast a swift glance into the shadows, but there was nothing distinctive – no shop, no movement, nothing but a double line of dull, flat-faced houses, a double stretch of wet flagstones which gleamed in the lamplight, and a double rush of water in the gutters which swirled and gurgled towards the sewer gratings. The door which faced them was blotched and discoloured, and a faint light in the fan pane above it served to show the dust and the grime which covered it. Above in one of the bedroom windows, there was a dull yellow glimmer. The merchant knocked loudly, and, as he turned his dark face towards the light, Douglas Stone could see that it was contracted with anxiety. A bolt was drawn, and an elderly woman with a taper stood in the doorway, shielding the thin flame with her gnarled hand.

'Is all well?' gasped the merchant.

'She is as you left her, sir.'

'She has not spoken?'

'No, she is in a deep sleep.'

The merchant closed the door, and Douglas Stone walked down the narrow passage, glancing about him in some surprise as he did so. There was no oil cloth, no mat, no hat rack. Deep grey dust and heavy festoons of cobwebs met his eyes everywhere. Following the old woman up the winding stair, his firm footfall echoed harshly through the silent house. There was no carpet.

The bedroom was on the second landing. Douglas Stone followed the old nurse into it, with the merchant at his heels. Here, at least, there was furniture and to spare. The floor was littered and the corners piled with Turkish cabinets, inlaid tables, coats of chain mail, strange pipes, and grotesque weapons. A single small lamp stood upon a bracket on the wall. Douglas Stone took it down, and picking his way among the lumber, walked over to a couch in the corner, on which lay a woman dressed in the Turkish fashion, with yashmak and veil. The lower part of the face was exposed, and the surgeon saw a jagged cut which zigzagged along the border of the under lip.

'You will forgive the yashmak,' said the Turk. 'You know our views about women in the East.'

But the surgeon was not thinking about the yashmak. This was no longer a woman to him. It was a case. He stooped and examined the wound carefully.

'There are no signs of irritation,' said he. 'We might delay the operation until local symptoms develop.'

The husband wrung his hands in uncontrollable agitation.

'Oh! Sir, sir,' he cried. 'Do not trifle. You do not know. It is deadly. I know, and I give you my assurance that an operation is absolutely necessary. Only the knife can save her.'

'And yet I am inclined to wait,' said Douglas Stone.

'That is enough,' the Turk cried, angrily. 'Every minute is of importance, and I cannot stand here and see my wife allowed to sink. It only remains for me to give you my thanks for having come, and to call in some other surgeon before it is too late.'

Douglas Stone hesitated. To refund that hundred pounds was no pleasant matter. But of course if he left the case he must return the money. And if the Turk were right and the woman died, his position before a coroner might be an embarrassing one.

'You have had personal experience of this poison?' he asked.

'I have.'

'And you assure me that an operation is needful.'

'I swear it by all that I hold sacred.'

'The disfigurement will be frightful.'

'I can understand that the mouth will not be a pretty one to kiss.'

Douglas Stone turned fiercely upon the man. The speech was a brutal one. But the Turk has his own fashion of talk and of thought, and there was no time for wrangling. Douglas Stone drew a bistoury from his case, opened it and felt the keen straight edge with his forefinger. Then he held the lamp closer to the bed. Two dark eyes were gazing up at him through the slit in the yashmak. They were all iris, and the pupil was hardly to be seen.

'You have given her a very heavy dose of opium.'

'Yes, she has had a good dose.'

He glanced again at the dark eyes which looked straight at his own. They were dull and lustreless, but, even as he gazed, a little shifting sparkle came into them, and the lips quivered.

'She is not absolutely unconscious,' said he.

'Would it not be well to use the knife while it will be painless?'

The same thought had crossed the surgeon's mind. He grasped the wounded lip with his forceps, and with two swift cuts he took out a broad V-shaped piece. The woman sprang up on the couch with a dreadful gurgling scream. Her covering was torn from her face. It was a face that he knew. In spite of that protruding upper lip and that slobber of blood, it was a face that he knew. She kept on putting her hand up to the gap and screaming. Douglas Stone sat down at the foot of the couch with his knife and his forceps. The room was whirling round, and he had felt something go like a ripping seam behind his ear. A bystander would have said that his face was the more ghastly of the two. As in a dream, or as if he had been looking at something at the play, he was conscious that the Turk's hair and beard lay upon the table, and that Lord Sannox was leaning against the wall with his hand to his side, laughing silently. The screams had died away now, and the dreadful head had dropped back again upon the pillow, but Douglas Stone still sat motionless, and Lord Sannox still chuckled quietly to himself.

'It was really very necessary for Marion, this operation,' said he, 'not physically, but morally, you know, morally.'

Douglas Stone stooped for yards and began to play with the fringe of the coverlet. His knife tinkled down upon the ground, but he still held the forceps and something more.

'I had long intended to make a little example,' said Lord Sannox, suavely. 'Your note of Wednesday miscarried, and I have it here in my pocketbook. I took some pains in carrying out my idea. The wound, by the way, was from nothing more dangerous than my signet ring.'

He glanced keenly at his silent companion, and cocked the small revolver which he held in his coat pocket. But Douglas Stone was still picking at the coverlet.

'You see you have kept your appointment after all,' said Lord Sannox.

And at that Douglas Stone began to laugh. He laughed long and loudly. But Lord Sannox did not laugh now. Something like fear sharpened and hardened his features. He walked from the room, and he walked on tiptoe. The old woman was waiting outside.

'Attend to your mistress when she awakes,' said Lord Sannox.

Then he went down to the street. The cab was at the door, and the driver raised his hand to his hat.

'John,' said Lord Sannox, 'you will take the doctor home first. He will want leading downstairs, I think. Tell his butler that he has been taken ill at a case.'

'Very good, sir.'

'Then you can take Lady Sannox home.'

'And how about yourself, sir?'

'Oh, my address for the next few months will be Hotel di Roma, Venice. Just see that the letters are sent on. And tell Stevens to exhibit all the purple chrysanthemums next Monday, and to wire me the result.'

Lucky's Grove

H. Russell Wakefield

'And Loki begat Hel, Goddess of the Grave,
Fenris, the Great Wolf, and the Serpent,
Nidnogg, who lives beneath The Tree.'

Mr Braxton strolled with his land agent, Curtis, into the Great Barn.

'There you are,' said Curtis, in a satisfied tone, 'the finest little fir I ever saw, and the kiddies will never set eyes on a lovelier Christmas tree.'

Mr Braxton examined it; it stood twenty feet from huge green pot to crisp, straight peak, and was exquisitely sturdy, fresh and symmetrical.

'Yes, it's a beauty,' he agreed. 'Where did you find it?'

'In that odd little spinney they call Lucky's Grove in the long meadow near the river boundary.'

'Oh!' remarked Mr Braxton uncertainly. To himself he

was saying vaguely, 'He shouldn't have got it from there, of course he wouldn't realise it, but he shouldn't have got it from there.'

'Of course we'll replant it,' said Curtis, noticing his employer's diminished enthusiasm. 'It's a curious thing, but it isn't a young tree; it's apparently full-grown. Must be a dwarf variety, but I don't know as much about trees as I should like.'

Mr Braxton was surprised to find there was one branch of country lore on which Curtis was not an expert; for he was about the best-known man at his job in the British Isles. Pigs, bees, chickens, cattle, crops, running a shoot, he had mastered them one and all. He paid him two thousand a year with house and car. He was worth treble.

'I expect it's all right,' said Mr Braxton; 'it is just that Lucky's Grove is – is – well, "sacred" is perhaps too strong a word. Maybe I should have told you, but I expect it's all right.'

'That accounts for it then,' laughed Curtis. 'I thought there seemed some reluctance on the part of the men while we were yanking it up and getting it on the lorry. They handled it a bit gingerly; on the part of the older men, I mean; the youngsters didn't worry.'

'Yes, there would be,' said Mr Braxton. 'But never mind, it'll be back in a few days and it's a superb little tree. I'll bring Mrs Braxton along to see it after lunch,' and he strolled back into Abingdale Hall.

Fifty-five years ago Mr Braxton's father had been a labourer on this very estate, and in that year young Percy, aged eight, had got an errand boy's job in Oxford. Twenty years later he'd owned one small shop. Twenty-five years after that fifty big shops. Now, though he had finally retired, he owned 280 vast shops and was a millionaire whichever way you added it up. How had this happened? No one can quite answer such questions. Certainly he'd worked like a brigade of Trojans, but midnight oil has to burn in Aladdin's Lamp before it can transform ninepence into one million pounds. It was just that he asked no quarter from the unforgiving minute, but squeezed from it the fruit of others' many hours. Those like Mr Braxton seem to have their own time scale; they just say the word and up springs a fine castle of commerce, but the knowledge of that word cannot be imparted; it is as mysterious as the Logos. But all through his great labours he had been moved by one fixed resolve – to avenge his father – that fettered spirit – for he had been an able, intelligent man who had had no earthly chance of revealing the fact to the world. Always the categorical determination had blazed in his son's brain, 'I will own Abingdale Hall, and, where my father sweated, I will rule and be lord.' And of course it had happened. Fate accepts the dictates of such men as Mr Braxton, shrugs its shoulders, and leaves its revenge to Death. The Hall had come on the market just when he was about to retire, and with an odd delight, an obscure sense of homecoming, the native returned, and his riding boots, shooting boots, golf shoes, and all the many glittering guineas' worth, stamped in and obliterated the prints of his father's hobnails.

That was the picture he often re-visualised, the way it amused him to 'put it to himself', as he roamed his broad acres and surveyed the many glowing triumphs of his model husbandry.

Some credit was due to buxom, blithe and debonair Mrs Braxton, kindly, competent and innately adaptable. She was awaiting him in the morning room and they went in solitary state to luncheon. But it was the last peaceful lunch they would have for a spell – 'The Families' were pouring in on the morrow.

As a footman was helping them to *sole meunière* Mr Braxton said, 'Curtis has found a very fine Christmas tree. It's in the barn. You must come and look at it after lunch.'

'That *is* good,' replied his wife. 'Where did he get it from?'

Mr Braxton hesitated for a moment.

'From Lucky's Grove.'

Mrs Braxton looked up sharply.

'From the grove!' she said, surprised.

'Yes, of course he didn't realise – anyway it'll be all right, it's all rather ridiculous, and it'll be replanted before the New Year.'

'Oh, yes,' agreed Mrs Braxton. 'After all it's only a clump of trees.'

'Quite. And it's just the right height for the ballroom. It'll be taken in there tomorrow morning and the electricians will work on it in the afternoon.'

'I heard from Lady Pounser just now,' said Mrs Braxton. 'She's bringing six over, that'll make seventy-four; only two refusals. The presents are arriving this afternoon.'

They discussed the party discursively over the cutlets and *pêche Melba* and soon after lunch walked across to the barn. Mr Braxton waved to Curtis, who was examining a new tractor in the garage fifty yards away, and he came over.

Mrs Braxton looked the tree over and was graciously

delighted with it, but remarked that the pot could have done with another coat of paint. She pointed to several streaks, rust-coloured, running through the green. 'Of course it won't show when it's wrapped, but they didn't do a very good job.'

Curtis leant down. 'They certainly didn't,' he answered irritably. 'I'll see to it. I think it's spilled over from the soil; that copse is on a curious patch of red sand – there are some at Frilford too. When we pulled it up I noticed the roots were stained a dark crimson.' He put his hand down and scraped at the stains with his thumb. He seemed a shade puzzled.

'It shall have another coat at once,' he said. 'What did you think of Lampson and Colletts' scheme for the barn?'

'Quite good,' replied Mrs Braxton, 'but the sketches for the chairs are too fancy.'

'I agree,' said Curtis, who usually did so in the case of unessentials, reserving his tactful vetoes for the others.

The Great Barn was by far the most aesthetically satisfying as it was the oldest feature of the Hall buildings: it was vast, exquisitely proportioned and mellow. That could hardly be said of the house itself, which the 4th Baron of Abingdale had rebuilt on the cinders of its predecessor in 1752.

This nobleman had travelled abroad extensively and returned with most enthusiastic, grandiose and indigestible ideas of architecture. The result was a gargantuan piece of rococo-jocoso which only an entirely humourless pedant could condemn. It contained forty-two bedrooms and eighteen reception rooms – so Mrs Braxton had made it at the last recount. But Mr Braxton had not repeated with the interior the errors of the 4th Baron. He'd briefed the greatest expert in Europe with the result that that interior was quite tasteful and sublimely comfortable.

'Ugh!' he exclaimed, as they stepped out into the air, 'it *is* getting nippy!'

'Yes,' said Curtis, 'there's a nor'-easter blowing up – may be snow for Christmas.'

On getting back to the house Mrs Braxton went into a huddle with butler and housekeeper and Mr Braxton retired to his study for a doze. But instead his mind settled on Lucky's Grove. When he'd first seen it again after buying the estate, it seemed as if fifty years had rolled away, and he realised that Abingdale was far more summed up to him in the little copse than in the gigantic barracks two miles away. At once he felt at home again. Yet, just as when he'd been a small boy, the emotion the grove had aroused in him had been sharply tinged with awe, so it had been now, half a century later. He still had a sneaking dread of it. How precisely he could see it, glowing darkly in the womb of the fire before him, standing starkly there in the centre of the big, fallow field, a perfect circle; and first, a ring of holm-oaks and, facing east, a breach therein to the firs and past them on the west a gap to the yews. It had always required a tug at his courage – not always forthcoming – to pass through them and face the mighty Scotch fir, rearing up its great bole from the grass mound. And when he stood before it, he'd always known an odd longing to fling himself down and – well, worship – it was the only word – the towering tree. His father had told him his forebears had done that very thing, but always when alone and at certain seasons of the year; and that no bird or beast was ever seen there. A lot of traditional nonsense, no doubt, but he himself had absorbed the spirit of the place and knew it would always be so.

One afternoon in late November, a few weeks after they had moved in, he'd gone off alone in the drowsing misty dark; and when he'd reached the holm-oak bastion and seen the great tree surrounded by its sentinels, he'd known again that quick turmoil of confused emotions. As he'd walked slowly towards it, it had seemed to quicken and be aware of his coming. As he passed the shallow grassy fosse and entered the oak ring he felt there was something he ought to say, some greeting, password or prayer. It was the most aloof, silent little place under the sun, and oh, so old. He'd tiptoed past the firs and faced the barrier of yews. He'd stood there for a long musing minute, tingling with the sensation that he was being watched and regarded. At length he stepped forward and stood before the God – that mighty word came abruptly and unforeseen – and he felt a wild desire to fling himself down on the mound and do obeisance. And then he'd hurried home. As he recalled all this most vividly and minutely, he was seized with a sudden gust of uncontrollable anger at the thought of the desecration of the grove. He knew now that if he'd had the slightest idea of Curtis's purpose he'd have resisted and opposed it. It was too late now. He realised he'd 'worked himself up' rather absurdly. What could it matter! He was still a superstitious bumpkin at heart. Anyway it was no fault of Curtis. It was the finest Christmas tree anyone could hope for, and the whole thing was too nonsensical for words. The general tone of these cadentic conclusions did not quite accurately represent his thoughts – a very rare failing with Mr Braxton.

About dinner time the blizzard set furiously in, and the snow was flying.

'Chains on the cars tomorrow,' Mrs Braxton told the head chauffeur.

'Boar's Hill'll be a beggar,' thought that person.

Mr and Mrs Braxton dined early, casually examined the presents, and went to bed. Mr Braxton was asleep at once as usual, but was awakened by the beating of a blind which had slipped its moorings. Reluctantly he got out of bed and went to fix it. As he was doing so he became conscious of the frenzied hysterical barking of a dog. The sound, muffled by the gale, came, he judged, from the barn. He believed the underkeeper kept his whippet there. Scared by the storm, he supposed, and returned to bed.

The morning was brilliantly fine and cold, but the snow-fall had been heavy.

'I heard a dog howling in the night, Perkins,' said Mr Braxton to the butler at breakfast; 'Drake's I imagine. What's the matter with it?'

'I will ascertain, sir,' replied Perkins.

'It was Drake's dog,' he announced a little later, 'apparently something alarmed the animal, for when Drake went to let it out this morning, it appeared to be extremely fright-ened. When the barn door was opened, it took to its heels and, although Drake pursued it, it jumped into the river and Drake fears it was drowned.'

'Um,' said Mr Braxton, 'must have been the storm; whip-pets are nervous dogs.'

'So I understand, sir.'

'Drake was so fond of it,' said Mrs Braxton, 'though it always looked so naked and shivering to me.'

'Yes, madam,' agreed Perkins, 'it had that appearance.'

Soon after Mr Braxton sauntered out into the blinding glitter. Curtis came over from the garage. He was heavily muffled up.

'They've got the chains on all the cars,' he said. 'Very seasonable and all that, but farmers have another word for it.' His voice was thick and hoarse.

'Yes,' said Mr Braxton. 'You're not looking very fit.'

'Not feeling it. Had to get up in the night. Thought I heard someone trying to break into the house, thought I saw him, too.'

'Indeed,' said Mr Braxton. 'Did you see what he was like?'

'No,' replied Curtis uncertainly. 'It was snowing like the devil. Anyway, I got properly chilled to the marrow, skipping around in my nightie.'

'You'd better get to bed,' said Mr Braxton solicitously. He had affection and a great respect for Curtis.

'I'll stick it out today and see how I feel tomorrow. We're going to get the tree across in a few minutes. Can I borrow the two footmen? I want another couple of pullers and haulers.'

Mr Braxton consented, and went off on his favourite little stroll across the sparkling meadows to the river and the pool where the big trout set their cunning noses to the stream.

Half an hour later Curtis had mobilised his scratch team of sleeve-rolled assistants and, with Perkins steering and himself breaking, they got to grips with the tree and bore it like a camouflaged battering ram towards the ballroom, which occupied the left centre of the frenetic frontage of the ground floor. There was a good deal of bumping and boring and genial blasphemy before the tree was manoeuvred into the middle of the room and levered by rope and muscle into position. As it came up its pinnacle just cleared the ceiling. Sam, a cowman, whose ginger mob had been buried in the foliage for some time, exclaimed tartly as he slapped the trunk, 'There ye are, ye old sod! Thanks for the scratches on me mug, ye old—!'

The next moment he was lying on his back, a livid weal across his right cheek.

This caused general merriment, and even Perkins permitted himself a spectral smile. There was more astonishment than pain on the face of Sam. He stared at the tree in a humble way for a moment, like a chastised and guilty dog, and then slunk from the room. The merriment of the others died away.

'More spring in these branches than you'd think,' said Curtis to Perkins.

'No doubt, sir, that is due to the abrupt release of the tension,' replied Perkins scientifically.

The 'Families' met at Paddington and travelled down together so at five o'clock three car-loads drew up at the Hall. There were Jack and Mary with Paddy aged eight, Walter and Pamela with Jane and Peter, seven and five respectively, and George and Gloria with Gregory and Phyllis, ten and eight.

Jack and Walter were sons of the house. They were much of a muchness, burly, handsome and as dominating as their sire; a fine pair of commercial kings, entirely capable rulers, but just lacking that something which founds dynasties. Their wives conformed equally to the social type to which they belonged, good-lookers, smart dressers, excellent wives and mothers, but rather coolly colourless, spiritually. Their offspring were 'charming children', flawless products of the English matrix, though Paddy showed signs of some obstreperous originality. 'George' was the Honourable George, Calvin, Roderick, et cetera Penables, and Gloria was Mr and Mrs Braxton's only daughter. George had inherited half a million and had started off at twenty-four to be something big in the City. In a sense he achieved his ambition, for two years later he was generally reckoned the biggest 'Something' in the City, from which he then withdrew, desperately clutching his last hundred thousand and vowing lachrymose repentance. He had kept his word and his wad, hunted and shot six days a week in the winter, and spent most of the summer wrestling with the two dozen devils in his golf bag. According to current jargon he was the complete extrovert, but what a relief are such, in spite of the pitying shrugs of those who for ever are peering into the septic recesses of their souls.

Gloria had inherited some of her father's force. She was rather overwhelmingly primed with energy and pep for her opportunities of releasing it. So she was always rather pent up and explosive, though maternity had kept the pressure down. She was dispassionately fond of George who had presented her with a nice little title and aristocratic background and two 'charming children'. Phyllis gave promise of such extreme beauty that, beyond being the cynosure of every press-camera's eye, and making a resounding match, no more was to be expected of her. Gregory, however, on the strength of some artistic precocity and a violent temper, was already somewhat prematurely marked down as a genius-to-be.

Such were the 'Families'.

During the afternoon four engineers arrived from one of the Braxton factories to fix up the lighting of the tree. The fairy lamps for this had been specially designed and executed for the occasion. Disney figures had been grafted upon them and made to revolve by an ingenious mechanism; the effect being to give the tree, when illuminated, an aspect of whirling life meant to be very cheerful and pleasing.

Mr Braxton happened to see these electricians departing in their lorry and noticed one of them had a bandaged arm and a rather white face. He asked Perkins what had happened.

'A slight accident, sir. A bulb burst and burnt him in some manner. But the injury is, I understand, not of a very serious nature.'

'He looked a bit white.'

'Apparently, sir, he got a fright, a shock of some kind, when the bulb exploded.'

After dinner the grown-ups went to the ballroom. Mr Braxton switched on the mechanism and great enthusiasm was shown. 'Won't the kiddies love it,' said George, grinning at the kaleidoscope. 'Look at the Big Bad Wolf. He looks so darn realistic I'm not sure I'd give him a "U" certificate.'

'It's almost frightening,' said Pamela, 'they look incredibly real. Daddie, you really are rather bright, darling.'

It was arranged that the work of decoration should be tackled on the morrow and finished on Christmas Eve.

'All the presents have arrived,' said Mrs Braxton, 'and are being unpacked. But I'll explain about them tomorrow.'

They went back to the drawing room. Presently Gloria puffed and remarked, 'Papa, aren't you keeping the house rather too hot?'

'I noticed the same thing,' said Mrs Braxton.

Mr Braxton walked over to a thermometer on the wall. 'You're right,' he remarked, 'seventy.' He rang the bell.

'Perkins,' he asked, 'who's on the furnace?'

'Churchill, sir.'

'Well, he's overdoing it. It's seventy. Tell him to get it back to fifty-seven.'

Perkins departed and returned shortly after.

'Churchill informs me he has damped down and cannot account for the increasing warmth, sir.'

'Tell him to get it back to fifty-seven at once,' rapped Mr Braxton.

'Very good, sir.'

'Open a window,' said Mrs Braxton.

'It is snowing again, madam.'

'Never mind.'

'My God!' exclaimed Mary, when she and Jack went up to bed. 'That furnace-man is certainly stepping on it. Open all the windows.'

A wild flurry of snow beat against the curtains.

Mr Braxton did what he very seldom did, woke up in the early hours. He awoke sweating from a furtive and demoralising dream. It had seemed to him that he had been crouching down in the fosse round Lucky's Grove and peering beneath the holm-oaks, and that there had been activity of a sort vaguely to be discerned therein, some quick, shadowy business. He knew a very tight terror at the thought of being detected at this spying, but he could not wrench himself away. That was all and he awoke still trembling and troubled. No wonder he'd had such a nightmare, the room seemed like a stokehold. He went to the windows and flung another open, and as he did so he glanced out. His room looked over the rock garden and down the path to the maze. Something moved just outside, it caught his eye. He thought he knew what it was, that big Alsatian which had been sheep-worrying in the neighbourhood. What an enormous brute. Or was it just because it was outlined against the snow? It vanished suddenly, apparently into the maze. He'd organise a hunt for it after Christmas; if the snow lay, it should be easy to track.

The first thing he did after breakfast was to send for Churchill, severely reprimand him and threaten him with dismissal from his ship. That person was almost tearfully insistent that he had obeyed orders and kept his jets low. 'I can't make it out, sir. It's got no right to be as 'ot as what it is.'

'That's nonsense!' said Mr Braxton. 'The system has been perfected and cannot take charge, as you suggest. See to it. You don't want me to get an engineer down, do you?'

'No, sir.'

'That's enough. Get it to fifty-seven and keep it there.'

Shortly after Mrs Curtis rang up to say her husband was quite ill with a temperature and that the doctor was coming. Mr Braxton asked her to ring him again after he'd been.

During the morning the children played in the snow. After a pitched battle in which the girls lost their tempers,

Gregory organised the erection of a snowman. He designed, the others fetched the material. He knew he had a reputation for brilliance to maintain and produce something Epsteinish, huge and squat. The other children regarded it with little enthusiasm, but, being Gregory, they supposed it must be admired. When it was finished Gregory wandered off by himself while the others went in to dry. He came in a little late for lunch during which he was silent and preoccupied. Afterwards the grown-ups sallied forth.

'Let's see your snowman, Greg,' said Gloria, in a mother-of-genius tone.

'It isn't all his, we helped,' said Phyllis, voicing a point of view which was to have many echoes in the coming years.

'Why, he's changed it!' exclaimed a chorus two minutes later.

'What an ugly thing!' exclaimed Mary, rather pleased at being able to say so with conviction.

Gregory had certainly given his imagination its head, for now the squat, inert truck was topped by a big wolf's head with open jaw and ears snarlingly laid back, surprisingly well modelled. Trailing behind it was a coiled, serpentine tail.

'Whatever gave you the idea for that?' asked Jack.

Usually Gregory was facile and eloquent in explaining his inspiration, but this time he refused to be drawn, bit his lip and turned away.

There was a moment's silence and then Gloria said with convincing emphasis, 'I think it's wonderful, Greg!'

And then they strolled off to examine the pigs and the poultry and the Suffolk punches.

They had just got back for tea when the telephone bell

rang in Mr Braxton's study. It was Mrs Curtis. The patient was no better and Dr Knowles had seemed rather worried, and so on. So Mr Braxton rang up the doctor.

'I haven't diagnosed his trouble yet,' he said. 'And I'm going to watch him carefully and take a blood test if he's not better tomorrow. He has a temperature of a hundred and two, but no other superficial symptoms, which is rather peculiar. By the way, one of your cowmen, Sam Colley, got a nasty wound on the face yesterday and shows signs of blood poisoning. I'm considering sending him to hospital. Some of your other men have been in to see me – quite a little outbreak of illness since Tuesday. However, I hope we'll have a clean bill again soon. I'll keep you informed about Curtis.'

Mr Braxton was one of those incredible people who never have a day's illness – till their first and last. Consequently his conception of disease was unimaginative and mechanical. If one of his more essential human machines was running unsatisfactorily, there was a machine-mender called a doctor whose business it was to ensure that all the plug leads were attached firmly and that the manifold drainpipe was not blocked. But he found himself beginning to worry about Curtis, and this little epidemic among his henchmen affected him disagreeably – there was something disturbing to his spirit about it. But just what and why, he couldn't analyse and decide.

After dinner, with the children out of the way, the business of decorating the tree was begun. The general scheme had been sketched out and coloured by one of the Braxton display experts and the company consulted this as they worked, which they did rather silently; possibly Mr Braxton's palpable anxiety somewhat affected them.

Pamela stayed behind after the others had left the ball-room to put some finishing touches to her section of the tree. When she rejoined the others she was looking rather white and tight-lipped. She said good night a shade abruptly and went to her room. Walter, a very, very good husband, quickly joined her.

'Anything the matter, old girl?' he asked anxiously.

'Yes,' replied Pamela, 'I'm frightened.'

'Frightened! What d'you mean?'

'You'll think it's all rot, but I'll tell you. When you'd all left the ballroom, I suddenly felt very uneasy – you know the sort of feeling when one keeps on looking round and can't concentrate. However, I stuck at it. I was a little way up the steps when I heard a sharp hiss from above me in the tree. I jumped back to the floor and looked up; now, of course, you won't believe me, but the trunk of the tree was moving – it was like the coils of a snake writhing upward, and there was something at the top of the tree, horrid-looking, peering at me. I know you won't believe me.'

Walter didn't, but he also didn't know what to make of it. 'I know what happened!' he improvised slightly. 'You'd been staring in at that trunk for nearly two hours and you got dizzy – like staring at the sun on the sea; and that snow dazzle this afternoon helped it. You've heard of snow-blind-ness – something like that, it still echoes from the retina or whatever …'

'You think it might have been that?'

'I'm sure of it.'

'And that horrible head?'

'Well, as George put it rather brightly, I don't think some

of those figures on the lamps should get a "U" certificate. There's the wolf to which he referred, and the witch.'

'Which witch?' laughed Pamela a little hysterically. 'I didn't notice one.'

'I did. I was working just near it, at least, I suppose it's meant to be a witch. A figure in black squinting round from behind a tree. As a matter of fact fairies never seemed all fun and frolic to me, there's often something diabolical about them – or rather casually cruel. Disney knows that.'

'Yes, there is,' agreed Pamela. 'So you think that's all there was to it?'

'I'm certain. One's eyes can play tricks on one.'

'Yes,' said Pamela, 'I know what you mean, as if they saw what one knew wasn't there or was different. Though who would "one" be then?'

'Oh, don't ask me that sort of question!' laughed Walter. 'Probably Master Gregory will be able to tell you in a year or two.'

'He's a nice little boy, really,' protested Pamela. 'Gloria just spoils him and it's natural.'

'I know he is, it's not his fault, but they will *force* him. Look at that snowman – and staying behind to do it. A foul-looking thing!'

'Perhaps his eyes played funny tricks with him,' said Pamela.

'What d'you mean by that?'

'I don't know why I said it,' said Pamela frowning. 'Sort of echo, I suppose. Let's go to bed.'

Walter kissed her gently but fervently, as he loved her. He was a one-lady's man and had felt a bit nervous about her for a moment or two.

Was the house a little cooler? wondered Mr Braxton, as he was undressing, or was it that he was getting more used to it? He was now convinced there was something wrong with the installation; he'd get an expert down. Meanwhile they must stick it. He yawned, wondered how Curtis was, and switched off the light.

Soon all the occupants were at rest and the great house swinging silently against the stars. *Should* have been at rest, rather, for one and all recalled that night with reluctance and dread. Their dreams were harsh and unhallowed, yet oddly related, being concerned with dim, uncertain and yet somehow urgent happenings in and around the house, as though some thing or things were stirring while they slept and communicated their motions to their dreaming consciousness. They awoke tired with a sense of unaccountable malaise.

Mrs Curtis rang up during breakfast and her voice revealed her distress. Timothy was delirious and much worse. The doctor was coming at 10.30.

Mr and Mrs Braxton decided to go over there, and sent for the car. Knowles was waiting just outside the house when they arrived.

'He's very bad,' he said quietly. 'I've sent for two nurses and Sir Arthur Galley; I want another opinion. Has he had some trouble with a tree?'

'Trouble with a tree!' said Mr Braxton, his nerves giving a flick.

'Yes, it's probably just a haphazard, irrational idea of delirium, but he continually fusses about some tree.'

'How bad is he?' asked Mrs Braxton.

The doctor frowned. 'I wish I knew. I'm fairly out of my depth. He's keeping up his strength fairly well, but he can't go on like this.'

'As bad as that!' exclaimed Mr Braxton.

'I'm very much afraid so. I'm anxiously awaiting Sir Arthur's verdict. By the way, that cowman is very ill indeed; I'm sending him into hospital.'

'What happened to him?' asked Mr Braxton, absently, his mind on Curtis.

'Apparently a branch of your Christmas tree snapped back at him and struck his face. Blood poisoning set in almost at once.'

Mr Braxton felt that tremor again, but merely nodded.

'I was just wondering if there might be some connection between the two, that Curtis is blaming himself for the accident. Seems an absurd idea, but judging from his ravings he appears to think he is lashed to some tree and that the great heat he feels comes from it.'

They went into the house and did their best to comfort and reassure Mrs Curtis, instructed Knowles to ring up as soon as Sir Arthur's verdict was known, and then drove home.

The children had just come in from playing in the snow.

'Grandpa, the snowman's melted,' said Paddy, 'did it thaw in the night?'

'Must have done,' replied Mr Braxton, forcing a smile.

'Come and look, Grandpa,' persisted Paddy, 'there's nothing left of it.'

'Grandpa doesn't want to be bothered,' said Mary, noticing his troubled face.

'I'll come,' said Mr Braxton. When he reached the site of

the snowman his thoughts were still elsewhere, but his mind quickly refocused itself, for he was faced with something a little strange. Not a vestige of the statue remained, though the snow was frozen crisp and crunched hard beneath their feet; and yet that snowman was completely obliterated and where it had stood was a circle of bare, brown grass.

'It must have thawed in the night and then frozen again,' he said uncertainly.

'Then why—' began Paddy.

'Don't bother Grandpa,' said Mary sharply. 'He's told you what happened.'

They wandered off towards the heavy, hurrying river.

'Are those dog-paw marks?' asked Phyllis.

That reminded Mr Braxton. He peered down. 'Yes,' he replied. 'And I bet they're those of that brute of an Alsatian; it must be a colossal beast.'

'And it must have paws like a young bear,' laughed Mary. 'They're funny dogs, sort of Jekyll and Hydes. I rather adore them.'

'You wouldn't adore this devil. He's all Hyde.' (I'm in the wrong mood for these festivities, he thought irritably.)

During the afternoon George and Walter took the kids to a cinema in Oxford; the others finished the decoration of the tree.

The presents, labelled with the names of their recipients, were arranged on tables round the room and the huge cracker, ten feet long and forty inches in circumference, was placed on its gaily decorated trestle near the tree. Just as the job was finished, Mary did a three-quarters faint, but was quickly revived with brandy.

'It's the simply ghastly heat in the house!' exclaimed Gloria, who was not looking too grand herself. 'The installation must be completely diseased. Ours always works perfectly.' Mary had her dinner in bed and Jack came up to her immediately he had finished his.

'How are you feeling, darling?' he asked.

'Oh, I'm all right.'

'It *was* just the heat, of course?'

'Oh, yes,' replied Mary with rather forced emphasis.

'Scared you a bit, going off like that?' suggested Jack, regarding her rather sharply.

'I'm quite all right, thank you,' said Mary in the tone she always adopted when she'd had enough of a subject. 'I'd like to rest. Switch off the light.'

But when Jack had gone, she didn't close her eyes, but lay on her back staring up at the faint outline of the ceiling. She frowned and lightly chewed the little finger of her left hand, a habit of hers when unpleasantly puzzled. Mary, like most people of strong character and limited imagination, hated to be puzzled. Everything she considered ought to have a simple explanation if one tried hard enough to find it. But how could one explain this odd thing that had happened to her? Besides the grandiose gifts on the tables which bore a number, as well as the recipient's name, a small present for everyone was hung on the tree. This also bore a number, the same one as the lordly gift, so easing the Braxtons' task of handing these out to the right people. Mary had just fixed Curtis's label to a cigarette lighter and tied it on the tree when it swung on its silk thread, so that the back of the card was visible; and on it was this inscription: 'Died, December

25th, 1938.' It spun away again and back and the inscription was no longer there.

Now Mary came of a family which rather prided itself on being unimaginative. Her father had confined his flights of fancy to the Annual Meeting of his shareholders, while to her mother, imagination and mendacity were at least first cousins. So Mary could hardly credit the explanation that, being remotely worried about Mr Curtis, she had subconsciously concocted that sinister sentence. On the other hand she knew poor Mr Curtis was very ill and, therefore, perhaps, if her brain had played that malign little trick on her, it might have done so in 'tombstone writing'.

This was a considerable logical exercise for Mary, the effort tired her, the impression began to fade and she started wondering how much longer Jack was going to sit up. She dozed off and there, as if flashed on the screen 'inside her head' was 'Died, December 25th, 1938.' This, oddly enough, completely reassured her. There was 'nothing there' this time. There had been nothing that other time. She'd been very weak and imaginative even to think otherwise.

While she was deciding this, Dr Knowles rang up. 'Sir Arthur has just been,' he said. 'And I'm sorry to say he's pessimistic. He says Curtis is very weak.'

'But what's the matter with him?' asked Mr Braxton urgently.

'He doesn't know. He calls it PUO, which really means nothing.'

'But what's it stand for?'

'Pyrexia unknown origin. There are some fevers which cannot be described more precisely.'

'How ill is he really?'

'All I can say is, we must hope for the best.'

'My God!' exclaimed Mr Braxton. 'When's Sir Arthur coming again?'

'At eleven tomorrow. I'll ring you up after he's been.'

Mr Braxton excused himself and went to his room. Like many men of his dominating, sometimes ruthless type, he was capable of an intensity of feeling, anger, resolution, desire for revenge, but also affection and sympathy, unknown to more superficially Christian and kindly souls. He was genuinely attached to Curtis and his wife and very harshly and poignantly moved by this news which, he realised, could hardly have been worse. He would have to exercise all his willpower if he was to sleep.

If on the preceding night the rest of the sleepers had been broken by influences which had insinuated themselves into their dreams, that which caused the night of that Christmas Eve to be unforgettable was the demoniacal violence of the elements. The northeaster had been waxing steadily all the evening and by midnight reached hurricane force, driving before it an almost impenetrable wall of snow. Not only so, but continually all through the night the wall was enflamed, and the roar of the hurricane silenced, by fearful flashes of lightning and claps of thunder. The combination was almost intolerably menacing. As the great house shook from the gale and trembled at the blasts and the windows blazed with strange polychromatic balls of flame, all were tense and troubled. The children fought or succumbed to their terror according to their natures; their parents soothed and reassured them.

Mr Braxton was convinced the lightning conductors were

struck three times within ten minutes, and he could imagine them recoiling from the mighty impacts and seething from the terrific charges. Not till a dilatory, chaotic dawn staggered up the sky did the storm temporarily lull. For a time the sky cleared and the frost came hard. It was a yawning and haggard company which assembled at breakfast. But determined efforts were made to engender a communal cheerfulness. Mr Braxton did his best to contribute his quota of seasonal bonhomie, but his mind was plagued by thoughts of Curtis. Before the meal was finished the vicar rang up to say the church tower had been struck and almost demolished, so there could be no services. It rang again to say that Brent's farmhouse had been burnt to the ground.

While the others went off to inspect the church Mr Braxton remained in his study. Presently Knowles rang to say Sir Arthur had been and pronounced Curtis weaker, but his condition was not quite hopeless. One of the most ominous symptoms was the violence of the delirium. Curtis appeared to be in great terror and sedatives had no effect.

'How's that cowman?' asked Mr Braxton.

'He died in the night, I'm sorry to say.'

Whereupon Mr Braxton broke one of his strictest rules by drinking a very stiff whisky with very little soda.

Christmas dinner was tolerably hilarious, and after it, the children, bulging and incipiently bilious, slept some of it off, while their elders put the final touches to the preparations for the party.

In spite of the weather, not a single 'cry-off' was telephoned. There was a good reason for this, Mr Braxton's entertainments were justly famous.

So from four-thirty onwards the 'Cream of North Berkshire Society' came ploughing through the snow to the Hall; Lady Pounser and party bringing up the rear in her heirloom Rolls which was dribbling steam from its ancient and aristocratic beak. A tea of teas, not merely a high tea, an Everest tea, towering, skyscraping, was then attacked by the already stuffed juveniles who, by the end of it, were almost livid with repletion, finding even the efforts of cracker-pulling almost beyond them.

They were then propelled into the library where rows of chairs had been provided for them. There was a screen at one end of the room, a projector at the other. Mr Braxton had provided one of his famed surprises! The room was darkened and on the screen was flashed the sentence: '*The North Berks News Reel.*'

During the last few weeks Mr Braxton had had a sharp-witted and discreetly furtive cameraman at work shooting some of the guests while busy about their more or less lawful occasions.

For example, there was a sentence from a speech by Lord Gallen, the Socialist peer: 'It is a damnable and calculated lie for our opponents to suggest we aim at a preposterous and essentially *inequitable* equalisation of income—' And then there was His Lordship just entering his limousine, and an obsequious footman, rug in hand, holding the door open for him.

His Lordship's laughter was raucous and vehement, though he *would* have liked to have said a few words in rebuttal.

And there was Lady Pounser's Rolls, locally known as

'the hippogriff', stuck in a snowdrift and enveloped in steam, with the caption, 'Oh, Mr Mercury, *do* give me a start!' And other kindly, slightly sardonic japes at the expense of the North Berks Cream.

The last scene was meant as an appropriate prelude to the climax of the festivities. It showed Curtis and his crew digging up the tree from Lucky's Grove. Out they came from the holm-oaks straining under their load, but close observers noticed there was one who remained behind, standing menacing and motionless, a very tall, dark, brooding figure. There came a blinding lightning flash which seemed to blaze sparking round the room and a fearsome metallic bang. The storm had returned with rasping and imperious salute.

The lights immediately came on and the children were marshalled into the ballroom. As they entered and saw the high tree shining there and the little people so lively upon its branches a prolonged 'O—h!' of astonishment was exhorted from the blasé brats. But there was another wave of flame against the windows which rattled wildly at the ensuing roar, and the cries of delight were tinged with terror. And, indeed, the hard, blue glare flung a sinister glow on the tree and its whirling throng.

The grown-ups hastened to restore equanimity and, forming rings of children, circled round the tree.

Presently Mrs Braxton exclaimed: 'Now then, look for your names on the cards and see what Father Christmas has brought you.'

Though hardly one of the disillusioned infants retained any belief in that superannuated Deliverer of Goods, the response was immediate. For they had sharp ears which had eagerly absorbed the tales of Braxton munificence. (At the same time it was noticeable that some approached the tree with diffidence, almost reluctance, and started back as a livid flare broke against the window blinds and the dread peals shook the streaming snow from the eaves.)

Mary had just picked up little Angela Rayner so that she could reach her card, when the child screamed out and pulled away her hand.

'The worm!' she cried, and a thick, black-grey squirming maggot fell from her fingers to the floor and writhed away. George, who was near, put his shoe on it with a squish.

One of the Pounser tribe, whose card was just below the Big Bad Wolf, refused to approach it. No wonder, thought Walter, for it looked horribly hunting and alive. There were other mischances too. The witch behind the sombre tree seemed to pounce out at Clarissa Balder, so she tearfully complained, and Gloria had to pull off her card for her. Of course Gregory was temperamental, seeming to stare at a spot just below the taut peak of the tree, as if mazed and entranced. But the presents were wonderful and more than worth the small ordeal of finding one's card and pretending not to be frightened when the whole room seemed full of fiery hands and the thunder cracked against one's eardrums and shook one's teeth. Easy to be afraid!

At length the last present had been bestowed and it was time for the *pièce de résistance*, the pulling of the great cracker. Long, silken cords streamed from each end with room among them for fifty chubby fists, and a great surprise inside, for sure. The languid, uneasy troop were lined up at each end and took a grip on the silken cords.

At that moment a footman came in and told Mr Braxton he was wanted on the telephone.

Filled with foreboding he went to his study. He heard the voice of Knowles:

'I'm afraid I have very bad news for you ...'

The chubby fists gripped the silken cords.

'Now pull!' cried Mrs Braxton.

The opposing teams took the strain.

A leaping flash and a blasting roar. The children were hurled, writhing and screaming over each other.

Up from the middle of the cracker leapt a rosy shaft of flame which, as it reached the ceiling, seemed to flatten its peak so that it resembled a great snake of fire which turned and hurled itself against the tree in a blinding embrace. There was a fierce sustained 'hiss', the tree flamed like a torch, and all the fairy globes upon it burst and splintered. And then the roaring torch cast itself down among the screaming chaos. For a moment the great pot, swathed in green, was a carmine cauldron and its paint streamed like blood upon the floor. Then the big room was a dream of fire and those within it driven wildly from its heat.

Phil Tangler, whose farmhouse, on the early slopes of Missen Rise, overlooked both Lucky's Grove and the Hall, solemnly declared that at 19.30 on Christmas Day, 1938, he was watching from a window and marvelling at the dense and boiling race of snow, the bitter gale, and the wicked flame and fury of the storm, when he saw a high fist of fire form in a rift in the cloud-rack, a fist with two huge blazing fingers, one of which speared down on the Hall, another touched and kindled the towering fir in Lucky's Grove, as though saluting it. Five minutes later he was racing through the hurricane to join in a vain night-long fight to save the Hall, already blazing from stem to stern.

The Story of a
Disappearance and
an Appearance

M. R. James

The letters which I now publish were sent to me recently by a person who knows me to be interested in ghost stories. There is no doubt about their authenticity. The paper on which they are written, the ink, and the whole external aspect put their date beyond the reach of question.

The only point which they do not make clear is the identity of the writer. He signs with initials only, and as none of the envelopes of the letters are preserved, the surname of his correspondent – obviously a married brother – is as obscure as his own. No further preliminary explanation is needed, I think. Luckily the first letter supplies all that could be expected.

LETTER I

GREAT CHRISHALL, Dec. 22, 1837.
MY DEAR ROBERT, – It is with great regret for the enjoy-
ment I am losing, and for a reason which you will deplore
equally with myself, that I write to inform you that I am
unable to join your circle for this Christmas: but you will
agree with me that it is unavoidable when I say that I have
within these few hours received a letter from Mrs Hunt at
B—, to the effect that our Uncle Henry has suddenly and
mysteriously disappeared, and begging me to go down there
immediately and join the search that is being made for him.
Little as I, or you either, I think, have ever seen of Uncle, I
naturally feel that this is not a request that can be regarded
lightly, and accordingly I propose to go to B— by this afternoon's mail, reaching it late in the evening. I shall not go to
the Rectory, but put up at the King's Head, and to which
you may address letters. I enclose a small draft, which you
will please make use of for the benefit of the young people.
I shall write you daily (supposing me to be detained more
than a single day) what goes on, and you may be sure, should
the business be cleared up in time to permit of no coming to
the Manor after all, I shall present myself. I have but a few
minutes at disposal. With cordial greetings to you all, and
many regrets, believe me, your affectionate Bro.,

W. R.

LETTER II

KING'S HEAD, Dec. 23, '37.
MY DEAR ROBERT, – In the first place, there is as yet

no news of Uncle H., and I think you may finally dismiss any idea – I won't say hope – that I might after all 'turn up' for Xmas. However, my thoughts will be with you, and you have my best wishes for a really festive day. Mind that none of my nephews or nieces expend any fraction of their guineas on presents for me.

Since I got here I have been blaming myself for taking this affair of Uncle H. too easily. From what people here say, I gather that there is very little hope that he can still be alive; but whether it is accident or design that carried him off I cannot judge. The facts are these. On Friday the 19th, he went as usual shortly before five o'clock to read evening prayers at the church; and when they were over the clerk brought him a message, in response to which he set off to pay a visit to a sick person at an outlying cottage the better part of two miles away. He paid the visit, and started on his return journey at about half past six. This is the last that is known of him. The people here are very much grieved at his loss; he had been here many years, as you know, and though, as you also know, he was not the most genial of men, and had more than a little of the *martinet* in his composition, he seems to have been active in good works, and unsparing of trouble to himself.

Poor Mrs Hunt, who has been his housekeeper ever since she left Woodley, is quite overcome: it seems like the end of the world to her. I am glad that I did not entertain the idea of taking quarters at the Rectory; and I have declined several kindly offers of hospitality from people in the place, preferring as I do to be independent, and finding myself very comfortable here.

You will, of course, wish to know what has been done in the way of inquiry and search. First, nothing was to be expected from investigation at the Rectory; and to be brief, nothing has transpired. I asked Mrs Hunt – as others had done before – whether there was either any unfavourable symptom in her master such as might portend a sudden stroke, or attack of illness, or whether he had ever had reason to apprehend any such thing: but both she, and also his medical man, were clear that this was not the case. He was quite in his usual health. In the second place, naturally, ponds and streams have been dragged, and fields in the neighbourhood which he is known to have visited last, have been searched – without result. I have myself talked to the parish clerk and – more important – have been to the house where he paid his visit.

There can be no question of any foul play on these people's part. The one man in the house is ill in bed and very weak: the wife and the children of course could do nothing themselves, nor is there the shadow of a probability that they or any of them should have agreed to decoy poor Uncle H. out in order that he might be attacked on the way back. They had told what they knew to several other inquirers already, but the woman repeated it to me. The Rector was looking just as usual: he wasn't very long with the sick man – 'He ain't,' she said, 'like some what has a gift in prayer; but there, if we was all that way, 'owever would the chapel people get their living?' He left some money when he went away, and one of the children saw him cross the stile into the next field. He was dressed as he always was: wore his bands – I gather he is nearly the last man remaining who does so – at any rate in this district.

You see I am putting down everything. The fact is that I have nothing else to do, having brought no business papers with me; and, moreover, it serves to clear my own mind, and may suggest points which have been overlooked. So I shall continue to write all that passes, even to conversations if need be – you may read or not as you please, but pray keep the letters. I have another reason for writing so fully, but it is not a very tangible one.

You may ask if I have myself made any search in the fields near the cottage. Something – a good deal – has been done by others, as I mentioned; but I hope to go over the ground tomorrow. Bow Street has now been informed, and will send down by tonight's coach, but I do not think they will make much of the job. There is no snow, which might have helped us. The fields are all grass. Of course I was on the *qui vive* for any indication today both going and returning; but there was a thick mist on the way back, and I was not in trim for wandering about unknown pastures, especially on an evening when bushes looked like men, and a cow lowing in the distance might have been the last trump. I assure you, if Uncle Henry had stepped out from among the trees in a little copse which borders the path at one place, carrying his head under his arm, I should have been very little more uncomfortable than I was. To tell you the truth, I was rather expecting something of the kind. But I must drop my pen for the moment: Mr Lucas, the curate, is announced.

Later. Mr Lucas has been, and gone, and there is not much beyond the decencies of ordinary sentiment to be got from him. I can see that he has given up any idea that the Rector can be alive, and that, so far as he can be, he is truly sorry. I can also discern that even in a more emotional person than Mr Lucas, Uncle Henry was not likely to inspire strong attachment.

Besides Mr Lucas, I have had another visitor in the shape of my Boniface – mine host of the 'King's Head' – who came to see whether I had everything I wished, and who really requires the pen of a Boz to do him justice. He was very solemn and weighty at first. 'Well, sir,' he said, 'I suppose we must bow our 'ead beneath the blow, as my poor wife had used to say. So far as I can gather there's been neither hide nor yet hair of our late respected incumbent scented out as yet; not that he was what the Scripture terms a hairy man in any sense of the word.'

I said – as well as I could – that I supposed not, but could not help adding that I had heard he was sometimes a little difficult to deal with. Mr Bowman looked at me sharply for a moment, and then passed in a flash from solemn sympathy to impassioned declamation. 'When I think', he said, 'of the language that man see fit to employ to me in this here parlour over no more a matter than a cask of beer – such a thing as I told him might happen any day of the week to a man with a family – though as it turned out he was quite under a mistake, and that I knew at the time, only I was that shocked to hear him I couldn't lay my tongue to the right expression.'

He stopped abruptly and eyed me with some embarrassment. I only said, 'Dear me, I'm sorry to hear you had any little differences: I suppose my uncle will be a good deal missed in the parish?' Mr Bowman drew a long breath. 'Ah, yes!' he said; 'your uncle! You'll understand me when I say that for the moment it had slipped my remembrance that he was a relative; and natural enough, I must say, as it should, for as to you bearing any resemblance to – to him, the notion of any such a thing is clean ridiculous. All the same, 'ad I 'ave bore it in my mind, you'll be among the first to feel, I'm sure, as I should have abstained my lips, or rather I should *not* have abstained my lips with no such reflections.'

I assured him that I quite understood, and was going to have asked him some further questions, but he was called away to see after some business. By the way, you need not take it into your head that he has anything to fear from the inquiry into poor Uncle Henry's disappearance – though, no doubt, in the watches of the night it will occur to him that *I* think he has, and I may expect explanations tomorrow. I must close this letter: it has to go by the late coach.

LETTER III

Dec. 25, '37.

MY DEAR ROBERT, – This is a curious letter to be writing on Christmas Day, and yet after all there is nothing much in it. Or there may be – you shall be the judge. At least, nothing decisive. The Bow Street men practically say that they have no clue. The length of time and the weather conditions have made all tracks so faint as to be quite useless: nothing that belonged to the dead man – I'm afraid no other word will do – has been picked up.

As I expected, Mr Bowman was uneasy in his mind this morning; quite early I heard him holding forth in a very distinct voice – purposely so, I thought – to the Bow Street officers in the bar, as to the loss that the town had sustained in their Rector, and as to the necessity of leaving no stone unturned (he was very great on this phrase) in order to come at the truth. I suspect him of being an orator of repute at convivial meetings.

When I was at breakfast he came to wait on me, and took an opportunity when handing a muffin to say in a low tone, 'I 'ope, sir, you reconise as my feelings towards your relative is not actuated by any taint of what you may call melignity – you can leave the room, Elizar, I will see the gentleman 'as all he requires with my own hands – I ask your pardon, sir, but you must be well aware a man is not always master of himself: and when that man has been 'urt in his mind by the application of expressions which I will go so far as to say 'ad not ought to have been made use of (his voice was rising all this time and his face growing redder); no, sir; and 'ere, if you will permit of it, I should like to explain to you in a very few words the exact state of the bone of contention. This cask – I might more truly call it a firkin – of beer—'

I felt it was time to interpose, and said that I did not see that it would help us very much to go into that matter in detail. Mr Bowman acquiesced, and resumed more calmly:

'Well, sir, I bow to your ruling, and as you say, be that here or be it there, it don't contribute a great deal, perhaps, to the present question. All I wish you to understand is that I am as prepared as you are yourself to lend every hand to the business we have afore us, and – as I took the opportunity to say as much to the Orficers not three quarters of an hour ago – to leave no stone unturned as may throw even a spark of light on this painful matter.'

In fact, Mr Bowman did accompany us on our exploration, but though I am sure his genuine wish was to be helpful, I am afraid he did not contribute to the serious side of it. He appeared to be under the impression that we were likely to meet either Uncle Henry or the person responsible for his disappearance, walking about the fields, and did a great deal of shading his eyes with his hand and calling our attention, by pointing with his stick to distant cattle and labourers. He held several long conversations with old women whom we met, and was very strict and severe in his manner, but on each occasion returned to our party saying, 'Well, I find she don't seem to 'ave no connexion with this sad affair. I think you may take it from me, sir, as there's little or no light to be looked for from that quarter; not without she's keeping somethink back intentional.'

We gained no appreciable result, as I told you at starting; the Bow Street men have left the town, whether for London or not I am not sure.

This evening I had company in the shape of a bagman, a smartish fellow. He knew what was going forward, but though he has been on the roads for some days about here, he had nothing to tell of suspicious characters – tramps, wandering sailors or gipsies. He was very full of a capital Punch and Judy Show he had seen this same day at W——, and asked if it had been here yet, and advised me by no means to miss it if it does come. The best Punch and the best Toby dog, he said, he had ever come across. Toby dogs, you know, are the last new thing in the shows. I have only seen one myself, but before long all the men will have them.

Now why, you will want to know, do I trouble to write all this to you? I am obliged to do it, because it has something to do with another absurd trifle (as you will inevitably say), which in my present state of rather unquiet fancy – nothing more, perhaps – I have to put down. It is a dream, sir, which I am going to record, and I must say it is one of the oddest I have had. Is there anything in it beyond what the bagman's talk and Uncle Henry's disappearance could have suggested? You, I repeat, shall judge: I am not in a sufficiently cool and judicial frame to do so.

It began with what I can only describe as a pulling aside of curtains: and I found myself seated in a place – I don't know whether indoors or out. There were people – only a few – on either side of me, but I did not recognise them, or indeed think much about them. They never spoke, but, so far as I remember, were all grave and pale-faced and looked fixedly before them. Facing me there was a Punch and Judy Show, perhaps rather larger than the ordinary ones, painted with black figures on a reddish-yellow ground. Behind it and on each side was only darkness, but in front there was a sufficiency of light. I was 'strung up' to a high degree of expectation and looked every moment to hear the pan-pipes and the Roo-too-too-it. Instead of that there came suddenly an enormous – I can use no other word – an enormous single toll of a bell, I don't know from how far off – somewhere behind. The little curtain flew up and the drama began.

I believe someone once tried to rewrite Punch as a serious tragedy; but whoever he may have been, this performance would have suited him exactly. There was something Satanic about the hero. He varied his methods of attack: for some of his victims he lay in wait, and to see his horrible face – it was yellowish white, I may remark – peering round the wings made me think of the Vampyre in Fuseli's foul sketch.

To others he was polite and carneying – particularly to the unfortunate alien who can only say *Shallabalah* – though what Punch said I never could catch. But with all of them I came to dread the moment of death. The crack of the stick on their skulls, which in the ordinary way delights me, had here a crushing sound as if the bone was giving way, and the victims quivered and kicked as they lay. The baby – it sounds more ridiculous as I go on – the baby, I am sure, was alive. Punch wrung its neck, and if the choke or squeak which it gave were not real, I know nothing of reality.

The stage got perceptibly darker as each crime was consummated, and at last there was one murder which was done quite in the dark, so that I could see nothing of the victim, and took some time to effect. It was accompanied by hard breathing and horrid muffled sounds, and after it Punch came and sat on the foot-board and fanned himself and looked at his shoes, which were bloody, and hung his head on one side, and sniggered in so deadly a fashion that I saw some of those beside me cover their faces, and I would gladly have done the same. But in the meantime the scene behind Punch was clearing, and showed, not the usual house front, but something more ambitious – a grove of trees and the gentle slope of a hill, with a very natural – in fact, I should say a real – moon shining on it. Over this there rose slowly an object which I soon perceived to be a human figure with something peculiar about the head – what, I was unable at first to see. It did not stand on its feet, but began creeping or dragging itself across the middle distance towards Punch, who still sat back to it; and by this time, I may remark (though it did not occur to me at the moment) that all pretence of this being a puppet show had vanished. Punch was still Punch, it is true, but, like the others, was in some sense a live creature, and both moved themselves at their own will.

When I next glanced at him he was sitting in malignant reflection; but in another instant something seemed to attract his attention, and he first sat up sharply and then turned round, and evidently caught sight of the person that was approaching him and was in fact now very near. Then, indeed, did he show unmistakable signs of terror: catching up his stick, he rushed towards the wood, only just eluding the arm of his pursuer, which was suddenly flung out to intercept him. It was with a revulsion which I cannot easily express that I now saw more or less clearly what this pursuer was like. He was a sturdy figure clad in black, and, as I thought, wearing bands: his head was covered with a whitish bag.

The chase which now began lasted I do not know how long, now among the trees, now along the slope of the field, sometimes both figures disappearing wholly for a few seconds, and only some uncertain sounds letting one know that they were still afoot. At length there came a moment when Punch, evidently exhausted, staggered in from the left and threw himself down among the trees. His pursuer was not long after him, and came looking uncertainly from side to side. Then, catching sight of the figure on the ground, he too threw himself down – his back was turned to the audience – with a swift motion twitched the covering from his head, and thrust his face into that of Punch. Everything on the instant grew dark.

There was one long, loud, shuddering scream, and I awoke to find myself looking straight into the face of – what in all the world do you think? but – a large owl, which was seated on my windowsill immediately opposite my bed foot, holding up its wings like two shrouded arms. I caught the fierce glance of its yellow eyes, and then it was gone. I heard the single enormous bell again – very likely, as you are saying to yourself, the church clock; but I do not think so – and then I was broad awake.

All this, I may say, happened within the last half hour. There was no probability of my getting to sleep again, so I got up, put on clothes enough to keep me warm, and am writing this rigmarole in the first hours of Christmas Day. Have I left out anything? Yes; there was no Toby dog, and the names over the front of the Punch and Judy booth were Kidman and Gallop, which were certainly not what the bagman told me to look out for. By this time, I feel a little more as if I could sleep, so this shall be sealed and wafered.

LETTER IV

Dec. 26, '37.

MY DEAR ROBERT, – All is over. The body has been found. I do not make excuses for not having sent off my news by last night's mail, for the simple reason that I was incapable of putting pen to paper. The events that attended the discovery bewildered me so completely that I needed what I could get of a night's rest to enable me to face the situation at all. Now I can give you my journal of the day, certainly the strangest Christmas Day that ever I spent or am likely to spend.

The first incident was not very serious. Mr Bowman had, I think, been keeping Christmas Eve, and was a little inclined to be captious: at least, he was not on foot very early, and to judge from what I could hear, neither men nor maids could do anything to please him. The latter were certainly reduced to tears; nor am I sure that Mr Bowman succeeded in preserving a manly composure. At any rate, when I came downstairs, it was in a broken voice that he wished me the compliments of the season, and a little later on, when he paid his visit of ceremony at breakfast, he was far from cheerful: even Byronic, I might almost say, in his outlook on life.

'I don't know', he said, 'if you think with me, sir; but every Christmas as comes round the world seems a hollerer thing to me. Why, take an example now from what lays under my own eye. There's my servant Eliza – been with me now for going on fifteen years. I thought I could have placed my confidence in Eliza, and yet this very morning – Christmas morning too, of all the blessed days in the year – with the bells a-ringing and – and – all like that – I say, this very morning, had it not have been for Providence watching over us all, that girl would have put – indeed I may go so far to say, 'ad put the cheese on your breakfast table—' He saw I was about to speak, and waved his hand at me. 'It's all very well for you to say, "Yes, Mr Bowman, but you took away the cheese and locked it up in the cupboard", which I did, and have the key here, or if not the actual key, one very much about the same size. That's true enough, sir, but what do you think is the effect of that action on me? Why, it's no exaggeration for me to say that the ground is cut from under my feet. And yet when I said as much to Eliza, not nasty, mind you, but just firm-like, what was my return? "Oh," she says: "well," she says, "there wasn't no bones broke, I suppose."

Well, sir, it 'urt me, that's all I can say: it 'urt me, and I don't like to think of it now.'

There was an ominous pause here, in which, I ventured to say something like, 'Yes, very trying,' and then asked at what hour the church service was to be. 'Eleven o'clock,' Mr Bowman said with a heavy sigh. 'Ah, you won't have no such discourse from poor Mr Lucas as what you would have done from our late Rector. Him and me may have had our little differences, and did do, more's the pity.' I could see that a powerful effort was needed to keep him off the vexed question of the cask of beer, but he made it. 'But I will say this, that a better preacher, nor yet one to stand faster by his rights, or what he considered to be his rights – however, that's not the question now – I for one, never set under. Some might say, "Was he a eloquent man?" and to that my answer would be: "Well, there you've a better right per'aps to speak of your own uncle than what I have." Others might ask, "Did he keep a hold of his congregation?' and there again I should reply, "That depends." But as I say – yes, Eliza, my girl, I'm coming – eleven o'clock, sir, and you inquire for the King's Head pew.' I believe Eliza had been very near the door, and shall consider it in my vail.

The next episode was church: I felt Mr Lucas had a difficult task in doing justice to Christmas sentiments, and also to the feeling of disquiet and regret which, whatever Mr Bowman might say, was clearly prevalent. I do not think he rose to the occasion. I was uncomfortable. The organ wolved – you know what I mean: the wind died – twice in the Christmas Hymn, and the tenor bell, I suppose owing to some negligence on the part of the ringers, kept sounding faintly about once in a minute during the sermon. The clerk sent up a man to see to it, but he seemed unable to do much. I was glad when it was over. There was an odd incident, too, before the service. I went in rather early, and came upon two men carrying the parish bier back to its place under the tower. From what I overheard them saying, it appeared that it had been put out by mistake, by someone who was not there. I also saw the clerk busy folding up a moth-eaten velvet pall – not a sight for Christmas Day.

I dined soon after this, and then, feeling disinclined to go out, took my seat by the fire in the parlour, with the last number of *Pickwick*, which I had been saving up for some days. I thought I could be sure of keeping awake over this, but I turned out as bad as our friend Smith. I suppose it was half past two when I was roused by a piercing whistle and laughing and talking voices outside in the marketplace. It was a Punch and Judy – I had no doubt the one that my bagman had seen at W——. I was half delighted, half not – the latter because my unpleasant dream came back to me so vividly; but, anyhow, I determined to see it through, and I sent Eliza out with a crown-piece to the performers and a request that they would face my window if they could manage it.

The show was a very smart new one; the names of the proprietors, I need hardly tell you, were Italian, Foresta and Calpigi. The Toby dog was there, as I had been led to expect. All B—— turned out, but did not obstruct my view, for I was at the large first-floor window and not ten yards away.

The play began on the stroke of a quarter to three by the church clock. Certainly it was very good; and I was soon relieved to find that the disgust my dream had given me for Punch's onslaughts on his ill-starred visitors was only transient. I laughed at the demise of the Turncock, the Foreigner, the Beadle, and even the baby. The only drawback was the Toby dog's developing a tendency to howl in the wrong place. Something had occurred, I suppose, to upset him, and something considerable: for, I forget exactly at what point, he gave a most lamentable cry, leapt off the foot-board, and shot away across the marketplace and down a side street. There was a stage-wait, but only a brief one. I suppose the men decided that it was no good going after him, and that he was likely to turn up again at night.

We went on. Punch dealt faithfully with Judy, and in fact with all comers; and then came the moment when the gallows was erected, and the great scene with Mr Ketch was to be enacted. It was now that something happened of which I can certainly not yet see the import fully. You have witnessed an execution, and know what the criminal's head looks like with the cap on. If you are like me, you never wish to think of it again, and I do not willingly remind you of it. It was just such a head as that, that I, from my somewhat higher post, saw in the inside of the show-box; but at first the audience did not see it. I expected it to emerge into their view, but instead of that there slowly rose for a few seconds an uncovered face, with an expression of terror upon it, of which I have never imagined the like. It seemed as if the man, whoever he was, was being forcibly lifted, with his arms somehow pinioned or held back, towards the little gibbet on the stage. I could just see the nightcapped head behind him. Then there was a cry and a crash. The whole show-box fell over backwards; kicking legs were seen among the ruins, and then two figures – as some said; I can only answer for one – were visible running at top speed across the square and disappearing in a lane which leads to the fields.

Of course everybody gave chase. I followed; but the pace was killing, and very few were in, literally, at the death. It happened in a chalk pit: the man went over the edge quite blindly and broke his neck. They searched everywhere for the other, until it occurred to me to ask whether he had ever left the marketplace. At first everyone was sure that he had; but when we came to look, he was there, under the show-box, dead too.

But in the chalk pit it was that poor Uncle Henry's body was found, with a sack over the head, the throat horribly mangled. It was a peaked corner of the sack sticking out of the soil that attracted attention. I cannot bring myself to write in greater detail.

I forgot to say the men's real names were Kidman and Gallop. I feel sure I have heard them, but no one here seems to know anything about them.

I am coming to you as soon as I can after the funeral. I must tell you when we meet what I think of it all.

The Book

Margaret Irwin

On a foggy night in November, Mr Corbett, having guessed the murderer by the third chapter of his detective story, arose in disappointment from his bed and went downstairs in search of something more satisfactory to send him to sleep.

The fog had crept through the closed and curtained windows of the dining room and hung thick on the air in a silence that seemed as heavy and breathless as the fog. The atmosphere was more choking than in his room, and very chill, although the remains of a large fire still burned in the grate.

The dining-room bookcase was the only considerable one in the house and held a careless unselected collection to suit all the tastes of the household, together with a few dull and obscure old theological books that had been left over from the sale of a learned uncle's library. Cheap red novels, bought on railway stalls by Mrs Corbett, who thought a journey the only time to read, were thrust in like pert, undersized intruders among the respectable nineteenth-century works of culture, chastely bound in dark blue or green, which Mr Corbett had considered the right thing to buy during his Oxford days; beside these there swaggered the children's large gaily bound story books and collections of Fairy Tales in every colour.

From among this neat new cloth-bound crowd there towered here and there a musty sepulchre of learning, brown with the colour of dust rather than leather, with no trace of gilded letters, however faded, on its crumbling back to tell what lay inside. A few of these moribund survivors from the Dean's library were inhospitably fastened with rusty clasps; all remained closed, and appeared impenetrable, their blank, forbidding backs uplifted above their frivolous surroundings with the air of scorn that belongs to a private and concealed knowledge. For only the worm of corruption now bored his way through their evil-smelling pages.

It was an unusual flight of fancy for Mr Corbett to imagine that the vaporous and fog-ridden air that seemed to hang more thickly about the bookcase was like a dank and poisonous breath exhaled by one or other of these slowly rotting volumes. Discomfort in this pervasive and impalpable presence came on him more acutely than at any time that day; in an attempt to clear his throat of it he choked most unpleasantly.

He hurriedly chose a Dickens from the second shelf as appropriate to a London fog, and had returned to the foot of the stairs when he decided that his reading tonight should by contrast be of blue Italian skies and white statues, in beautiful rhythmic sentences. He went back for a Walter Pater.

He found *Marius the Epicurean* tipped sideways across the gap left by his withdrawal of *The Old Curiosity Shop*. It was a very wide gap to have been left by a single volume, for the books on that shelf had been closely wedged together. He put the Dickens back into it and saw that there was still space for a large book. He said to himself in careful and precise words: 'This is nonsense. No one can possibly have gone into the dining room and removed a book while I was crossing the hall. There must have been a gap before in the second shelf.' But another part of his mind kept saying in a hurried, tumbled torrent: 'There was no gap in the second shelf. There was no gap in the second shelf.'

He snatched at both the *Marius* and *The Old Curiosity Shop*, and went to his room in a haste that was unnecessary and absurd, since even if he believed in ghosts, which he did not, no one had the smallest reason for suspecting any in the modern Kensington house wherein he and his family had lived for the last fifteen years. Reading was the best thing to calm the nerves, and Dickens a pleasant, wholesome and robust author.

Tonight, however, Dickens struck him in a different light. Beneath the author's sentimental pity for the weak and helpless, he could discern a revolting pleasure in cruelty and suffering, while the grotesque figures of the people in Cruikshank's illustrations revealed too clearly the hideous distortions of their souls. What had seemed humorous now appeared diabolic, and in disgust at these two favourites he turned to Walter Pater for the repose and dignity of a classic spirit.

But presently he wondered if this spirit were not in itself of a marble quality, frigid and lifeless, contrary to the purpose of nature. 'I have often thought', he said to himself, 'that there is something evil in the austere worship of beauty for its own sake.' He had never thought so before, but he liked to think that this impulse of fancy was the result of mature consideration, and with this satisfaction he composed himself for sleep.

He woke two or three times in the night, an unusual occurrence, but he was glad of it, for each time he had been dreaming horribly of these blameless Victorian works. Sprightly devils in whiskers and peg-top trousers tortured a lovely maiden and leered in delight at her anguish; the gods and heroes of classic fable acted deeds whose naked crime and shame Mr Corbett had never appreciated in Latin and Greek Unseens. When he had woken in a cold sweat from the spectacle of the ravished Philomel's torn and bleeding tongue, he decided there was nothing for it but to go down and get another book that would turn his thoughts in some more pleasant direction. But his increasing reluctance to do this found a hundred excuses. The recollection of the gap in the shelf now occurred to him with a sense of unnatural importance; in the troubled dozes that followed, this gap between two books seemed the most hideous deformity, like a gap between the front teeth of some grinning monster.

But in the clear daylight of the morning Mr Corbett came down to the pleasant dining room, its sunny windows and smell of coffee and toast, and ate an undiminished breakfast with a mind chiefly occupied in self-congratulation that the wind had blown the fog away in time for his Saturday game of golf. Whistling happily, he was pouring out his final cup of coffee when his hand remained arrested in the act as his glance, roving across the bookcase, noticed that there was now no gap at all in the second shelf. He asked who had been at the bookcase already, but neither of the girls had, nor Dicky, and Mrs Corbett was not yet down. The maid never touched the books. They wanted to know what book he missed in it, which made him look foolish, as he could not say. The things that disturb us at midnight are negligible at 9 a.m.

'I thought there was a gap in the second shelf,' he said, 'but it doesn't matter.'

'There never is a gap in the second shelf,' said little Jean brightly. 'You can take out lots of books from it and when you go back the gap's always filled up. Haven't you noticed that? I have.'

Nora, the middle one in age, said Jean was always being silly; she had been found crying over the funny pictures in *The Rose and the Ring* because she said all the people in them had such wicked faces, and the picture of a black cat had upset her because she thought it was a witch. Mr Corbett did not like to think of such fancies for his Jeannie. She retaliated briskly by saying Dicky was just as bad, and he was a big boy. He had kicked a book across the room and said, 'Filthy stuff,' just like that. Jean was a good mimic; her tone expressed a venom of disgust, and she made the gesture of dropping a book as though the very touch of it were loathsome. Dicky, who had been making violent signs at her, now told her she was a beastly little sneak and he would never again take her for rides on the step of his bicycle. Mr Corbett was disturbed. Unpleasant housemaids and bad schoolfriends passed through his head, as he gravely asked his son how he had got hold of this book.

'Took it out of that bookcase of course,' said Dicky furiously.

It turned out to be the *Boy's Gulliver's Travels* that Granny had given him, and Dicky had at last to explain his rage with the devil who wrote it to show that men were worse than beasts and the human race a washout. A boy who never had good school reports had no right to be so morbidly sensitive as to penetrate to the underlying cynicism of Swift's delightful fable, and that moreover in the bright and carefully expurgated edition they bring out nowadays. Mr Corbett could not say he had ever noticed the cynicism himself, though he knew from the critical books it must be there, and with some annoyance he advised his son to take out a nice bright modern boy's adventure story that could not depress anybody. It appeared, however, that Dicky was 'off reading just now', and the girls echoed this.

Mr Corbett soon found that he too was 'off reading'. Every new book seemed to him weak, tasteless and insipid; while his old and familiar books were depressing or even, in some obscure way, disgusting. Authors must all be filthy-minded; they probably wrote what they dared not express in their lives. Stevenson had said that literature was a morbid secretion; he read Stevenson again to discover his peculiar morbidity, and detected in his essays a self-pity masquerading as courage, and in *Treasure Island* an invalid's sickly attraction to brutality.

This gave him a zest to find out what he disliked so much, and his taste for reading revived as he explored with relish the hidden infirmities of minds that had been valued by fools as great and noble. He saw Jane Austen and Charlotte Brontë as two unpleasant examples of spinsterhood; the one as a prying, sub-acid busybody in everyone else's flirtations, the other as a raving, craving maenad seeking self-immolation on the altar of her frustrated passions. He compared Wordsworth's love of nature to the monstrous egoism of an ancient bellwether, isolated from the flock.

These powers of penetration astonished him. With a mind so acute and original he should have achieved greatness, yet he was a mere solicitor and not prosperous at that. If he had but the money, he might do something with those ivory shares, but it would be a pure gamble, and he had no luck. His natural envy of his wealthier acquaintances now mingled with a contempt for their stupidity that approached loathing. The digestion of his lunch in the City was ruined by meeting sentimental yet successful dotards whom he had once regarded as pleasant fellows. The very sight of them spoiled his game of golf, so that he came to prefer reading alone in the dining room even on sunny afternoons.

He discovered also and with a slight shock that Mrs Corbett had always bored him. Dicky he began actively to dislike as an impudent blockhead, and the two girls were as insipidly alike as white mice; it was a relief when he abolished their tiresome habit of coming in to say good night.

In the now unbroken silence and seclusion of the dining room, he read with feverish haste as though he were seeking for some clue to knowledge, some secret key to existence which would quicken and inflame it, transform it from its present dull torpor to a life worthy of him and his powers.

He even explored the few decaying remains of his uncle's theological library. Bored and baffled, he yet persisted, and had the occasional relief of an ugly woodcut of Adam and Eve with figures like bolsters and hair like dahlias, or a map of the Cosmos with Hell-mouth in the corner, belching forth demons. One of these books had diagrams and symbols in the margin which he took to be mathematical formulae of a kind he did not know. He presently discovered that they were drawn, not printed, and that the book was in manuscript, in a very neat, crabbed black writing that resembled black-letter printing. It was moreover in Latin, a fact that gave Mr Corbett a shock of unreasoning disappointment. For while examining the signs in the margin, he had been filled with an extraordinary exultation as though he knew himself to be on the edge of a discovery that should alter his whole life. But he had forgotten his Latin.

With a secret and guilty air which would have looked absurd to anyone who knew his harmless purpose, he stole to the schoolroom for Dicky's Latin dictionary and grammar and hurried back to the dining room, where he tried to discover what the book was about with an anxious industry that surprised himself. There was no name to it, nor of the author. Several blank pages had been left at the end, and the writing ended at the bottom of a page, with no flourish or superscription, as though the book had been left unfinished. From what sentences he could translate, it seemed to be a work on theology rather than mathematics. There were constant references to the Master, to his wishes and injunctions, which appeared to be of a complicated kind. Mr Corbett began by skipping these as mere accounts of ceremonial, but a word caught his eye as one unlikely to occur in such an account. He read this passage attentively, looking up each word in the dictionary, and could hardly believe the result of his translation. 'Clearly,' he decided, 'this book must be by some early missionary, and the passage I have just read the account of some horrible rite practised by a savage tribe of devil-worshippers.' Though he called it 'horrible', he reflected on it, committing each detail to memory. He then amused himself by copying the signs in the margin near it and trying to discover their significance. But a sensation of sickly cold came over him, his head swam, and he could hardly see the figures before his eyes. He suspected a sudden attack of influenza, and went to ask his wife for medicine.

They were all in the drawing room, Mrs Corbett helping Nora and Jean with a new game, Dicky playing the pianola, and Mike, the Irish terrier, who had lately deserted his accustomed place on the dining-room hearth rug, stretched by the fire. Mr Corbett had an instant's impression of this peaceful and cheerful scene, before his family turned towards him and asked in scared tones what was the matter. He thought how like sheep they looked and sounded; nothing in his appearance in the mirror struck him as odd; it was their gaping faces that were unfamiliar. He then noticed the extraordinary behaviour of Mike, who had sprung from the hearth rug and was crouched in the furthest corner, uttering no sound, but with his eyes distended and foam round his bared teeth. Under Mr Corbett's glance, he slunk towards the door, whimpering in a faint and abject manner, and then as his master called him, he snarled horribly, and the hair bristled on the scruff of his neck. Dicky let him out, and they heard him scuffling at a frantic rate down the stairs to the kitchen, and then, again and again, a long-drawn howl.

'What *can* be the matter with Mike?' asked Mrs Corbett.

Her question broke a silence that seemed to have lasted a long time. Jean began to cry. Mr Corbett said irritably that he did not know what was the matter with any of them.

Then Nora asked, 'What is that red mark on your face?'

He looked again in the glass and could see nothing.

'It's quite clear from here,' said Dicky; 'I can see the lines in the fingerprint.'

'Yes, that's what it is,' said Mrs Corbett in her brisk staccato voice; 'the print of a finger on your forehead. Have you been writing in red ink?'

Mr Corbett precipitately left the room for his own, where he sent down a message that he was suffering from headache and would have his dinner in bed. He wanted no one fussing round him. By next morning he was amazed at his fancies of influenza, for he had never felt so well in his life.

No one commented on his looks at breakfast, so he concluded that the mark had disappeared. The old Latin book he had been translating on the previous night had been moved from the writing bureau, although Dicky's grammar and dictionary were still there. The second shelf was, as always in the daytime, closely packed; the book had, he remembered, been in the second shelf. But this time he did not ask who had put it back.

That day he had an unexpected stroke of luck in a new client of the name of Crab, who entrusted him with large sums of money: nor was he irritated by the sight of his more prosperous acquaintances, but with difficulty refrained from grinning in their faces, so confident was he that his remarkable ability must soon place him higher than any of them. At dinner he chaffed his family with what he felt to be the gaiety of a schoolboy. But on them it had a contrary effect, for they stared, either at him in stupid astonishment, or at their plates, depressed and nervous. Did they think him drunk? he wondered, and a fury came on him at their low and bestial suspicions and heavy dullness of mind. Why, he was younger than any of them! But in spite of this new alertness he could not attend to the letters he should have written that evening and drifted to the bookcase for a little light distraction, but found that for the first time there was nothing he wished to read. He pulled out a book from above his head at random, and saw that it was the old Latin book in manuscript. As he turned over its stiff and yellow pages, he noticed with pleasure the smell of corruption that had first repelled him in these decaying volumes, a smell, he now thought, of ancient and secret knowledge.

This idea of secrecy seemed to affect him personally, for on hearing a step in the hall he hastily closed the book and put it back in its place. He went to the schoolroom where Dicky was doing his homework, and told him he required his Latin grammar and dictionary again for an old law report. To his annoyance he stammered and put his words awkwardly; he thought that the boy looked oddly at him and he cursed him in his heart for a suspicious young devil, though of what he should be suspicious he could not say. Nevertheless, when back in the dining room, he listened at the door and then softly turned the lock before he opened the books on the writing bureau.

The script and Latin seemed much clearer than on the previous evening, and he was able to read at random a passage relating to a trial of a German midwife in 1620 for the murder and dissection of 783 children. Even allowing for the opportunities afforded by her profession, the number appeared excessive, nor could he discover any motive for the slaughter. He decided to translate the book from the beginning.

It appeared to be an account of some secret society whose activities and ritual were of a nature so obscure, and when not, so vile and terrible, that Mr Corbett would not at first believe that this could be a record of any human mind, although his deep interest in it should have convinced him that from his humanity at least it was not altogether alien.

He read until far later than his usual hour for bed and when at last he rose, it was with the book in his hands. To defer his parting with it, he stood turning over the pages until he reached the end of the writing, and was struck by a new peculiarity.

The ink was much fresher and of a far poorer quality than the thick rusted ink in the bulk of the book; on close inspection he would have said that it was of modern manufacture and written quite recently were it not for the fact that it was in the same crabbed late-seventeenth-century handwriting.

This, however, did not explain the perplexity, even dismay and fear, he now felt as he stared at the last sentence. It ran: 'Contine te in perennibus studiis', and he had at once recognised it as a Ciceronian tag that had been dinned into him at school. He could not understand how he had failed to notice it yesterday.

Then he remembered that the book had ended at the

bottom of a page. But now, the last two sentences were written at the very top of a page. However long he looked at them, he could come to no other conclusion than that they had been added since the previous evening.

He now read the sentence before the last: '*Re imperfecta mortuus sum*,' and translated the whole as: 'I died with my purpose unachieved. Continue, thou, the never-ending studies.'

With his eyes still fixed upon it, Mr Corbett replaced the book on the writing bureau and stepped back from it to the door, his hand outstretched behind him, groping and then tugging at the door handle. As the door failed to open, his breath came in a faint, hardly articulate scream. Then he remembered that he had himself locked it, and he fumbled with the key in frantic ineffectual movements until at last he opened it and banged it after him as he plunged backwards into the hall.

For a moment he stood there looking at the door handle; then with a stealthy, sneaking movement, his hand crept out towards it, touched it, began to turn it, when suddenly he pulled his hand away and went up to his bedroom, three steps at a time.

There he behaved in a manner only comparable with the way he had lost his head after losing his innocence when a schoolboy of sixteen. He hid his face in the pillow, he cried, he raved in meaningless words, repeating: 'Never, never, never. I will never do it again. Help me never to do it again.' With the words, 'Help me,' he noticed what he was saying, they reminded him of other words, and he began to pray aloud. But the words sounded jumbled, they persisted in coming into his head in a reverse order so that he found he was saying his prayers backwards, and at this final absurdity he suddenly began to laugh very loud. He sat up on the bed, delighted at this return to sanity, common sense and humour, when the door leading into Mrs Corbett's room opened, and he saw his wife staring at him with a strange, grey, drawn face that made her seem like the terror-stricken ghost of her usually smug and placid self.

'It's not burglars,' he said irritably. 'I've come to bed late, that is all, and must have waked you.'

'Henry,' said Mrs Corbett, and he noticed that she had not heard him, 'Henry, didn't you hear it?'

'What?'

'That laugh.'

He was silent, an instinctive caution warning him to wait until she spoke again. And this she did, imploring him with her eyes to reassure her.

'It was not a human laugh. It was like the laugh of a devil.'

He checked his violent inclination to laugh again. It was wiser not to let her know that it was only his laughter she had heard. He told her to stop being fanciful, and Mrs Corbett, gradually recovering her docility, returned to obey an impossible command, since she could not stop being what she had never been.

The next morning, Mr Corbett rose before any of the servants and crept down to the dining room. As before, the dictionary and grammar alone remained on the writing bureau; the book was back in the second shelf. He opened it at the end. Two more lines had been added, carrying the writing down to the middle of the page. They ran:

Ex auro canceris
In dentem elephantis.

which he translated as:

Out of the money of the crab
Into the tooth of the elephant.

From this time on, his acquaintances in the City noticed a change in the mediocre, rather flabby and unenterprising 'old Corbett'. His recent sour depression dropped from him: he seemed to have grown twenty years younger, strong, brisk and cheerful, and with a self-confidence in business that struck them as lunacy. They waited with a not unpleasant excitement for the inevitable crash, but his every speculation, however wild and hare-brained, turned out successful. He no longer avoided them, but went out of his way to display his consciousness of luck, daring and vigour, and to chaff them in a manner that began to make him actively disliked. This he welcomed with delight as a sign of others' envy and his superiority.

He never stayed in town for dinners or theatres, for he was always now in a hurry to get home, where, as soon as he was sure of being undisturbed, he would take down the manuscript book from the second shelf of the dining room and turn to the last pages.

Every morning he found that a few words had been added since the evening before, and always they formed, as he considered, injunctions to himself. These were at first only with regard to his money transactions, giving assurance to his boldest fancies, and since the brilliant and unforeseen success that had attended his gamble with Mr Crab's money in African ivory, he followed all such advice unhesitatingly.

But presently, interspersed with these commands, were others of a meaningless, childish, yet revolting character such as might be invented by a decadent imbecile, or, it must be admitted, by the idle fancies of any ordinary man who permits his imagination to wander unbridled. Mr Corbett was startled to recognise one or two such fancies of his own, which had occurred to him during his frequent boredom in church, and which he had not thought any other mind could conceive.

He at first paid no attention to these directions, but found that his new speculations declined so rapidly that he became terrified not merely for his fortune but for his reputation and even safety, since the money of various of his clients was involved. It was made clear to him that he must follow the commands in the book altogether or not at all, and he began to carry out their puerile and grotesque blasphemies with a contemptuous amusement, which, however, gradually changed to a sense of their monstrous significance. They became more capricious and difficult of execution, but he now never hesitated to obey blindly, urged by a fear that he could not understand, but knew only that it was not of mere financial failure.

By now he understood the effect of this book on the others near it, and the reason that had impelled its mysterious agent to move the books into the second shelf so that all in turn should come under the influence of that ancient and secret knowledge.

In respect to it, he encouraged his children, with jeers at

their stupidity, to read more, but he could not observe that they ever now took a book from the dining-room bookcase. He himself no longer needed to read, but went to bed early and slept sound. The things that all his life he had longed to do when he should have enough money now seemed to him insipid. His most exciting pleasure was the smell and touch of these mouldering pages as he turned them to find the last message inscribed to him.

One evening it was in two words only: '*Canem occide.*'

He laughed at this simple and pleasant request to kill the dog, for he bore Mike a grudge for his change from devotion to slinking aversion. Moreover, it could not have come more opportunely, since in turning out an old desk he had just discovered some packets of rat poison bought years ago and forgotten. No one therefore knew of its existence and it would be easy to poison Mike without any further suspicion than that of a neighbour's carelessness. He whistled light-heartedly as he ran upstairs to rummage for the packets, and returned to empty one in the dog's dish of water in the hall.

That night the household was awakened by terrified screams proceeding from the stairs. Mr Corbett was the first to hasten there, prompted by the instinctive caution that was always with him these days. He saw Jean, in her nightdress, scrambling up on to the landing on her hands and knees, clutching at anything that afforded support and screaming in a choking, tearless, unnatural manner. He carried her to the room she shared with Nora, where they were quickly followed by Mrs Corbett.

Nothing coherent could be got from Jean. Nora said that she must have been having her old dream again; when her

father demanded what this was, she said that Jean sometimes woke in the night, crying, because she had dreamed
of a hand passing backwards and forwards over the dining-
room bookcase, until it found a certain book and took it out
of the shelf. At this point she was always so frightened that
she woke up.

On hearing this, Jean broke into fresh screams, and Mrs
Corbett would have no more explanations. Mr Corbett went
out onto the stairs to find what had brought the child there
from her bed. On looking down into the lighted hall, he saw
Mike's dish overturned. He went down to examine it and
saw that the water he had poisoned must have been upset and
absorbed by the rough doormat, which was quite wet.

He went back to the little girls' room, told his wife that she
was tired and must go to bed, and he would take his turn at
comforting Jean. She was now much quieter. He took her
on his knee where at first she shrank from him. Mr Corbett
remembered with an angry sense of injury that she never
now sat on his knee, and would have liked to pay her out for
it by mocking and frightening her. But he had to coax her into
telling him what he wanted, and with this object he soothed
her, calling her by pet names that he thought he had forgotten,
telling her that nothing could hurt her now he was with her.

At first his cleverness amused him; he chuckled softly
when Jean buried her head in his dressing gown. But
presently an uncomfortable sensation came over him, he
gripped at Jean as though for her protection, while he was so
smoothly assuring her of his. With difficulty, he listened to
what he had at last induced her to tell him.

She and Nora had kept Mike with them all the evening and

taken him to sleep in their room for a treat. He had lain at the foot of Jean's bed and they had all gone to sleep. Then Jean began her old dream of the hand moving over the books in the dining-room bookcase; but instead of taking out a book, it came across the dining room and out on to the stairs. It came up over the banisters and to the door of their room, and turned their door handle very softly and opened it. At this point she jumped up wide awake and turned on the light, calling to Nora. The door, which had been shut when they went to sleep, was wide open, and Mike was gone. She told Nora that she was sure something dreadful would happen to him if she did not go and bring him back, and ran down into the hall where she saw him just about to drink from his dish. She called to him and he looked up, but did not come, so she ran to him, and began to pull him along with her, when her nightdress was clutched from behind and then she felt a hand seize her arm. She fell down, and then clambered upstairs as fast as she could, screaming all the way.

It was now clear to Mr Corbett that Mike's dish must have been upset in the scuffle. She was again crying, but this time he felt himself unable to comfort her. He retired to his room, where he walked up and down in an agitation he could not understand, for he found his thoughts perpetually arguing on a point that had never troubled him before.

'I am not a bad man,' he kept saying to himself. 'I have never done anything actually wrong. My clients are none the worse for my speculations, only the better. Nor have I spent my new wealth on gross and sensual pleasures; these now have even no attraction for me.'

Presently he added: 'It is not wrong to try and kill a dog,

an ill-tempered brute. It turned against me. It might have bitten Jeannie.'

He noticed that he had thought of her as Jeannie, which he had not done for some time; it must have been because he had called her that tonight. He must forbid her ever to leave her room at night, he could not have her meddling. It would be safer for him if she were not there at all.

Again that sick and cold sensation of fear swept over him: he seized the bedpost as though he were falling, and held on to it for some minutes. 'I was thinking of a boarding school,' he told himself, and then, 'I must go down and find out – find out—' He would not think what it was he must find out.

He opened his door and listened. The house was quiet. He crept onto the landing and along to Nora's and Jean's door where again he stood, listening. There was no sound, and at that he was again overcome with unreasonable terror. He imagined Jean lying very still in her bed, too still. He hastened away from the door, shuffling in his bedroom slippers along the passage and down the stairs.

A bright fire still burned in the dining-room grate. A glance at the clock told him it was not yet twelve. He stared at the bookcase. In the second shelf was a gap which had not been there when he had left. On the writing bureau lay a large open book. He knew that he must cross the room and see what was written in it. Then, as before, words that he did not intend came sobbing and crying to his lips, muttering, 'No, no, not that. Never, never, never.' But he crossed the room and looked down at the book. As last time, the message was in only two words: '*Infantem occide.*'

He slipped and fell forward against the bureau. His hands

clutched at the book, lifted it as he recovered himself and with his finger he traced out the words that had been written. The smell of corruption crept into his nostrils. He told himself that he was not a snivelling dotard, but a man stronger and wiser than his fellows, superior to the common emotions of humanity, who held in his hands the sources of ancient and secret power.

He had known what the message would be. It was after all the only safe and logical thing to do. Jean had acquired dangerous knowledge. She was a spy, an antagonist. That she was so unconsciously, that she was eight years old, his youngest and favourite child, were sentimental appeals that could make no difference to a man of sane reasoning power such as his own. Jean had sided with Mike against him. 'All that are not with me are against me,' he repeated softly. He would kill both dog and child with the white powder that no one knew to be in his possession. It would be quite safe.

He laid down the book and went to the door. What he had to do, he would do quickly, for again that sensation of deadly cold was sweeping over him. He wished he had not to do it tonight; last night it would have been easier, but tonight she had sat on his knee and made him afraid. He imagined her lying very still in her bed, too still. But it would be she who would lie there, not he, so why should he be afraid? He was protected by ancient and secret powers. He held on to the door handle, but his fingers seemed to have grown numb, for he could not turn it. He clung to it, crouched and shivering, bending over it until he knelt on the ground, his head beneath the handle which he still clutched with upraised hands. Suddenly the hands were loosened and flung outwards with the frantic gesture of a man falling from a great height, and he stumbled to his feet. He seized the book and threw it on the fire. A violent sensation of choking overcame him, he felt he was being strangled, as in a nightmare he tried again and again to shriek aloud, but his breath would make no sound. His breath would not come at all. He fell backwards heavily, down on the floor, where he lay very still.

In the morning, the maid who came to open the dining-room windows found her master dead. The sensation caused by this was scarcely so great in the City as that given by the simultaneous collapse of all Mr Corbett's recent speculations. It was instantly assumed that he must have had previous knowledge of this and so committed suicide.

The stumbling block to this theory was that the medical report defined the cause of Mr Corbett's death as strangulation of the windpipe by the pressure of a hand which had left the marks of its fingers on his throat.

The Kit-Bag

Algernon Blackwood

When the words 'Not Guilty' sounded through the crowded court room that dark December afternoon, Arthur Wilbraham, the great criminal KC, and leader for the triumphant defence, was represented by his junior: but Johnson, his private secretary, carried the verdict across to his chambers like lightning.

'It's what we expected, I think,' said the barrister, without emotion; 'and, personally, I am glad the case is over.' There was no particular sign of pleasure that his defence of John Turk, the murderer, on a plea of insanity, had been successful, for no doubt he felt, as everybody who had watched the case felt, that no man had ever better deserved the gallows.

'I'm glad too,' said Johnson. He had sat in the court for ten days watching the face of the man who had carried out with callous detail one of the most brutal and cold-blooded murders of recent years.

The counsel glanced up at his secretary. They were more than employer and employed; for family and other reasons, they were friends. 'Ah, I remember; yes,' he said with a kind smile, 'and you want to get away for Christmas? You're going to skate and ski in the Alps, aren't you? If I was your age I'd come with you.'

Johnson laughed shortly. He was a young man of twenty-six, with a delicate face like a girl's. 'I can catch the morning boat now,' he said; 'but that's not the reason I'm glad the trial is over. I'm glad it's over because I've seen the last of that man's dreadful face. It positively haunted me. That white skin, with the black hair brushed low over the forehead, is a thing I shall never forget, and the description of the way the dismembered body was crammed and packed with lime into that—'

'Don't dwell on it, my dear fellow,' interrupted the other, looking at him curiously out of his keen eyes, 'don't think about it. Such pictures have a trick of coming back when one least wants them.' He paused a moment. 'Now go,' he added presently, 'and enjoy your holiday. I shall want all your energy for my Parliamentary work when you get back. And don't break your neck skiing.'

Johnson shook hands and took his leave. At the door he turned suddenly.

'I knew there was something I wanted to ask you,' he said. 'Would you mind lending me one of your kit-bags? It's too late to get one tonight, and I leave in the morning before the shops are open.'

'Of course; I'll send Henry over with it to your rooms. You shall have it the moment I get home.'

'I promise to take great care of it,' said Johnson gratefully, delighted to think that within thirty hours he would be nearing the brilliant sunshine of the high Alps in winter. The thought of that criminal court was like an evil dream in his mind.

He dined at his club and went on to Bloomsbury, where he occupied the top floor in one of those old, gaunt houses in which the rooms are large and lofty. The floor below his own was vacant and unfurnished, and below that were other lodgers whom he did not know. It was cheerless, and he looked forward heartily to a change. The night was even more cheerless: it was miserable, and few people were about. A cold, sleety rain was driving down the streets before the keenest east wind he had ever felt. It howled dismally among the big, gloomy houses of the great squares, and when he reached his rooms he heard it whistling and shouting over the world of black roofs beyond his windows.

In the hall he met his landlady, shading a candle from the draughts with her thin hand. 'This come by a man from Mr Wilbr'im's, sir.'

She pointed to what was evidently the kit-bag, and Johnson thanked her and took it upstairs with him. 'I shall be going abroad in the morning for ten days, Mrs Monks,' he said. 'I'll leave an address for letters.'

'And I hope you'll 'ave a merry Christmas, sir,' she said, in a raucous, wheezy voice that suggested spirits, 'and better weather than this.'

'I hope so too,' replied her lodger, shuddering a little as the wind went roaring down the street outside.

When he got upstairs he heard the sleet volleying against

the windowpanes. He put his kettle on to make a cup of hot coffee, and then set about putting a few things in order for his absence. 'And now I must pack – such as my packing is,' he laughed to himself, and set to work at once.

He liked the packing, for it brought the snow mountains so vividly before him, and made him forget the unpleasant scenes of the past ten days. Besides, it was not elaborate in nature. His friend had lent him the very thing – a stout canvas kit-bag, sack-shaped, with holes round the neck for the brass bar and padlock. It was a bit shapeless, true, and not much to look at, but its capacity was unlimited, and there was no need to pack carefully. He shoved in his waterproof coat, his fur cap and gloves, his skates and climbing boots, his sweaters, snow boots and ear caps; and then on the top of these he piled his woollen shirts and underwear, his thick socks, puttees and knickerbockers. The dress suit came next, in case the hotel people dressed for dinner, and then, thinking of the best way to pack his white shirts, he paused a moment to reflect. 'That's the worst of these kit-bags,' he mused vaguely, standing in the centre of the sitting room, where he had come to fetch some string.

It was after ten o'clock. A furious gust of wind rattled the windows as though to hurry him up, and he thought with pity of the poor Londoners whose Christmas would be spent in such a climate, while he was skimming over snowy slopes in bright sunshine, and dancing in the evening with rosy-cheeked girls – Ah! that reminded him; he must put in his dancing pumps and evening socks. He crossed over from his sitting room to the cupboard on the landing where he kept his linen.

And as he did so he heard someone coming softly up the stairs.

He stood still a moment on the landing to listen. It was Mrs Monks's step, he thought; she must be coming up with the last post. But then the steps ceased suddenly, and he heard no more. They were at least two flights down, and he came to the conclusion they were too heavy to be those of his bibulous landlady. No doubt they belonged to a late lodger who had mistaken his floor. He went into his bedroom and packed his pumps and dress shirts as best he could.

The kit-bag by this time was two-thirds full, and stood upright on its own base like a sack of flour. For the first time he noticed that it was old and dirty, the canvas faded and worn, and that it had obviously been subjected to rather rough treatment. It was not a very nice bag to have sent him – certainly not a new one, or one that his chief valued. He gave the matter a passing thought, and went on with his packing. Once or twice, however, he caught himself wondering who it could have been wandering down below, for Mrs Monks had not come up with letters, and the floor was empty and unfurnished. From time to time, moreover, he was almost certain he heard a soft tread of someone padding about over the bare boards – cautiously, stealthily, as silently as possible – and, further, that the sounds had been lately coming distinctly nearer.

For the first time in his life he began to feel a little creepy. Then, as though to emphasise this feeling, an odd thing happened: as he left the bedroom, having just packed his recalcitrant white shirts, he noticed that the top of the kit-bag lopped over towards him with an extraordinary resemblance to a human face. The canvas fell into a fold like a nose and forehead, and the brass rings for the padlock just filled the position of the eyes. A shadow – or was it a travel stain? for he could not tell exactly – looked like hair. It gave him rather a turn, for it was so absurdly, so outrageously, like the face of John Turk, the murderer.

He laughed, and went into the front room, where the light was stronger.

'That horrid case has got on my mind,' he thought; 'I shall be glad of a change of scene and air.' In the sitting room, however, he was not pleased to hear again that stealthy tread upon the stairs, and to realise that it was much closer than before, as well as unmistakably real. And this time he got up and went out to see who it could be creeping about on the upper staircase at so late an hour.

But the sound ceased; there was no one visible on the stairs. He went to the floor below, not without trepidation, and turned on the electric light to make sure that no one was hiding in the empty rooms of the unoccupied suite. There was not a stick of furniture large enough to hide a dog. Then he called over the banisters to Mrs Monks, but there was no answer, and his voice echoed down into the dark vault of the house, and was lost in the roar of the gale that howled outside. Everyone was in bed and asleep – everyone except himself and the owner of this soft and stealthy tread.

'My absurd imagination, I suppose,' he thought. 'It must have been the wind after all, although – it seemed so *very* real and close, I thought.' He went back to his packing. It was by this time getting on towards midnight. He drank his coffee up and lit another pipe – the last before turning in.

It is difficult to say exactly at what point fear begins, when the causes of that fear are not plainly before the eyes. Impressions gather on the surface of the mind, film by film, as ice gathers upon the surface of still water, but often so lightly that they claim no definite recognition from the consciousness. Then a point is reached where the accumulated impressions become a definite emotion, and the mind realises that something has happened. With something of a start, Johnson suddenly recognised that he felt nervous – oddly nervous; also, that for some time past the causes of this feeling had been gathering slowly in his mind, but that he had only just reached the point where he was forced to acknowledge them.

It was a singular and curious malaise that had come over him, and he hardly knew what to make of it. He felt as though he were doing something that was strongly objected to by another person, another person, moreover, who had some right to object. It was a most disturbing and disagreeable feeling, not unlike the persistent promptings of conscience: almost, in fact, as if he were doing something he knew to be wrong. Yet, though he searched vigorously and honestly in his mind, he could nowhere lay his finger upon the secret of this growing uneasiness, and it perplexed him. More, it distressed and frightened him.

'Pure nerves, I suppose,' he said aloud with a forced laugh. 'Mountain air will cure all that! Ah,' he added, still speaking to himself, 'and that reminds me – my snow-glasses.'

He was standing by the door of the bedroom during this brief soliloquy, and as he passed quickly towards the sitting room to fetch them from the cupboard he saw out of the corner of his eye the indistinct outline of a figure standing on the stairs, a few feet from the top. It was someone in a stooping position, with one hand on the banisters, and the face peering up towards the landing. And at the same moment he heard a shuffling footstep. The person who had been creeping about below all this time had at last come up to his own floor. Who in the world could it be? And what in the name of Heaven did he want?

Johnson caught his breath sharply and stood stock still. Then, after a few seconds' hesitation, he found his courage, and turned to investigate. The stairs, he saw to his utter amazement, were empty; there was no one. He felt a series of cold shivers run over him, and something about the muscles of his legs gave a little and grew weak. For the space of several minutes he peered steadily into the shadows that congregated about the top of the staircase where he had seen the figure, and then he walked fast – almost ran, in fact – into the light of the front room; but hardly had he passed inside the doorway when he heard someone come up the stairs behind him with a quick bound and go swiftly into his bedroom. It was a heavy, but at the same time a stealthy footstep – the tread of somebody who did not wish to be seen. And it was at this precise moment that the nervousness he had hitherto experienced leaped the boundary line, and entered the state of fear, almost of acute, unreasoning fear. Before it turned into terror there was a further boundary to cross, and beyond that again lay the region of pure horror. Johnson's position was an unenviable one.

'By Jove! That *was* someone on the stairs, then,' he muttered, his flesh crawling all over; 'and whoever it was has now gone into my bedroom.' His delicate, pale face turned absolutely white, and for some minutes he hardly knew what to think or do. Then he realised intuitively that delay only set a premium upon fear; and he crossed the landing boldly and went straight into the other room, where, a few seconds before, the steps had disappeared.

'Who's there? Is that you, Mrs Monks?' he called aloud, as he went, and heard the first half of his words echo down the empty stairs, while the second half fell dead against the curtains in a room that apparently held no other human figure than his own.

'Who's there?' he called again, in a voice unnecessarily loud and that only just held firm. 'What do you want here?'

The curtains swayed very slightly, and, as he saw it, his heart felt as if it almost missed a beat; yet he dashed forward and drew them aside with a rush. A window, streaming with rain, was all that met his gaze. He continued his search, but in vain; the cupboards held nothing but rows of clothes, hanging motionless; and under the bed there was no sign of anyone hiding. He stepped backwards into the middle of the room, and, as he did so, something all but tripped him up. Turning with a sudden spring of alarm he saw – the kit-bag.

'Odd!' he thought. 'That's not where I left it!' A few moments before it had surely been on his right, between the bed and the bath; he did not remember having moved it. It was very curious. What in the world was the matter with everything? Were all his senses gone queer? A terrific gust of wind tore at the windows, dashing the sleet against the glass with the force of a small gunshot, and then fled away howling dismally over the waste of Bloomsbury roofs. A sudden vision of the Channel next day rose in his mind and recalled him sharply to realities.

'There's no one here at any rate; that's quite clear!' he exclaimed aloud. Yet at the time he uttered them he knew perfectly well that his words were not true and that he did not believe them himself. He felt exactly as though someone was hiding close about him, watching all his movements, trying to hinder his packing in some way. 'And two of my senses,' he added, keeping up the pretence, 'have played me the most absurd tricks: the steps I heard and the figure I saw were both entirely imaginary.'

He went back to the front room, poked the fire into a blaze, and sat down before it to think. What impressed him more than anything else was the fact that the kit-bag was no longer where he had left it. It had been dragged nearer to the door.

What happened afterwards that night happened, of course, to a man already excited by fear, and was perceived by a mind that had not the full and proper control, therefore, of the senses. Outwardly, Johnson remained calm and master of himself to the end, pretending to the very last that everything he witnessed had a natural explanation, or was merely delusions of his tired nerves. But inwardly, in his very heart, he knew all along that someone had been hiding downstairs in the empty suite when he came in, that this person had watched his opportunity and then stealthily made his way up to the bedroom, and that all he saw and heard afterwards, from the moving of the kit-bag to – well, to the other things this story has to tell – were caused directly by the presence of this invisible person.

And it was here, just when he most desired to keep his mind

and thoughts controlled, that the vivid pictures received day after day upon the mental plates exposed in the court room of the Old Bailey, came strongly to light and developed themselves in the dark room of his inner vision. Unpleasant, haunting memories have a way of coming to life again just when the mind least desires them – in the silent watches of the night, on sleepless pillows, during the lonely hours spent by sick and dying beds. And so now, in the same way, Johnson saw nothing but the dreadful face of John Turk, the murderer, lowering at him from every corner of his mental field of vision; the white skin, the evil eyes, and the fringe of black hair low over the forehead. All the pictures of those ten days in court crowded back into his mind unbidden, and very vivid.

'This is all rubbish and nerves,' he exclaimed at length, springing with sudden energy from his chair. 'I shall finish my packing and go to bed. I'm overwrought, overtired. No doubt, at this rate I shall hear steps and things all night!'

But his face was deadly white all the same. He snatched up his field-glasses and walked across to the bedroom, humming a music-hall song as he went – a trifle too loud to be natural; and the instant he crossed the threshold and stood within the room something turned cold about his heart, and he felt that every hair on his head stood up.

The kit-bag lay close in front of him, several feet nearer to the door than he had left it, and just over its crumpled top he saw a head and face slowly sinking down out of sight as though someone were crouching behind it to hide, and at the same moment a sound like a long-drawn sigh was distinctly audible in the still air about him between the gusts of the storm outside.

Johnson had more courage and willpower than the girlish indecision of his face indicated; but at first such a wave of terror came over him that for some seconds he could do nothing but stand and stare. A violent trembling ran down his back and legs, and he was conscious of a foolish, almost an hysterical, impulse to scream aloud. That sigh seemed in his very ear, and the air still quivered with it. It was unmistakably a human sigh.

'Who's there?' he said at length, finding his voice; but though he meant to speak with loud decision, the tones came out instead in a faint whisper, for he had partly lost the control of his tongue and lips.

He stepped forward, so that he could see all round and over the kit-bag. Of course there was nothing there, nothing but the faded carpet and the bulging canvas sides. He put out his hands and threw open the mouth of the sack where it had fallen over, being only three parts full, and then he saw for the first time that round the inside, some six inches from the top, there ran a broad smear of dull crimson. It was an old and faded blood stain. He uttered a scream, and drew back his hands as if they had been burnt. At the same moment the kit-bag gave a faint, but unmistakable, lurch forward towards the door.

Johnson collapsed backwards, searching with his hands for the support of something solid, and the door, being farther behind him than he realised, received his weight just in time to prevent his falling, and shut to with a resounding bang. At the same moment the swinging of his left arm accidentally touched the electric switch, and the light in the room went out.

It was an awkward and disagreeable predicament, and if Johnson had not been possessed of real pluck he might have done all manner of foolish things. As it was, however, he pulled himself together, and groped furiously for the little brass knob to turn the light on again. But the rapid closing of the door had set the coats hanging on it a-swinging, and his fingers became entangled in a confusion of sleeves and pockets, so that it was some moments before he found the switch. And in those few moments of bewilderment and terror two things happened that sent him beyond recall over the boundary into the region of genuine horror – he distinctly heard the kit-bag shuffling heavily across the floor in jerks, and close in front of his face sounded once again the sigh of a human being.

In his anguished efforts to find the brass button on the wall he nearly scraped the nails from his fingers, but even then, in those frenzied moments of alarm – so swift and alert are the impressions of a mind keyed up by a vivid emotion – he had time to realise that he dreaded the return of the light, and that it might be better for him to stay hidden in the merciful screen of darkness. It was but the impulse of a moment, however, and before he had time to act upon it he had yielded automatically to the original desire, and the room was flooded again with light.

But the second instinct had been right. It would have been better for him to have stayed in the shelter of the kind darkness. For there, close before him, bending over the half-packed kit-bag, clear as life in the merciless glare of the electric light, stood the figure of John Turk, the murderer. Not three feet from him the man stood, the fringe of black hair marked plainly against the pallor of the forehead, the whole horrible presentment of the scoundrel, as vivid as he had seen him day after day in the Old Bailey, when he stood there in the dock, cynical and callous, under the very shadow of the gallows.

In a flash Johnson realised what it all meant: the dirty and much-used bag; the smear of crimson within the top; the dreadful stretched condition of the bulging sides. He remembered how the victim's body had been stuffed into a canvas bag for burial, the ghastly, dismembered fragments forced with lime into this very bag; and the bag itself produced as evidence – it all came back to him as clear as day ...

Very softly and stealthily his hand groped behind him for the handle of the door, but before he could actually turn it the very thing that he most of all dreaded came about, and John Turk lifted his devil's face and looked at him. At the same moment that heavy sigh passed through the air of the room, formulated somehow into words: 'It's my bag. And I want it.'

Johnson just remembered clawing the door open, and then falling in a heap upon the floor of the landing, as he tried frantically to make his way into the front room.

He remained unconscious for a long time, and it was still dark when he opened his eyes and realised that he was lying, stiff and bruised, on the cold boards. Then the memory of what he had seen rushed back into his mind, and he promptly fainted again. When he woke the second time the wintry dawn was just beginning to peep in at the windows, painting the stairs a cheerless, dismal grey, and he managed to crawl into the front room, and cover himself with an overcoat in the armchair, where at length he fell asleep.

A great clamour woke him. He recognised Mrs Monks's voice, loud and voluble.

'What! You ain't been to bed, sir! Are you ill, or has anything 'appened? And there's an urgent gentleman to see you, though, it ain't seven o'clock yet, and—'

'Who is it?' he stammered. 'I'm all right, thanks. Fell asleep in my chair, I suppose.'

'Someone from Mr Wilbr'im's, and he says he ought to see you quick before you go abroad, and I told him—'

'Show him up, please, at once,' said Johnson, whose head was whirling, and his mind was still full of dreadful visions.

Mr Wilbraham's man came in with many apologies, and explained briefly and quickly that an absurd mistake had been made, and that the wrong kit-bag had been sent over the night before.

'Henry somehow got hold of the one that came over from the court room, and Mr Wilbraham only discovered it when he saw his own lying in his room, and asked why it had not gone to you,' the man said.

'Oh!' said Johnson stupidly.

'And he must have brought you the one from the murder case instead, sir, I'm afraid,' the man continued, without the ghost of an expression on his face. 'The one John Turk packed the dead body in. Mr Wilbraham's awful upset about it, sir, and told me to come over first thing this morning with the right one, as you were leaving by the boat.'

He pointed to a clean-looking kit-bag on the floor, which he had just brought. 'And I was to bring the other one back, sir,' he added casually.

For some minutes Johnson could not find his voice. At

last he pointed in the direction of his bedroom. 'Perhaps you would kindly unpack it for me. Just empty the things out on the floor.'

The man disappeared into the other room, and was gone for five minutes. Johnson heard the shifting to and fro of the bag, and the rattle of the skates and boots being unpacked.

'Thank you, sir,' the man said, returning with the bag folded over his arm. 'And can I do anything more to help you, sir?'

'What is it?' asked Johnson, seeing that he still had something he wished to say.

The man shuffled and looked mysterious. 'Beg pardon, sir, but knowing your interest in the Turk case, I thought you'd maybe like to know what's happened—'

'Yes.'

'John Turk killed himself last night with poison immediately on getting his release, and he left a note for Mr Wilbraham saying as he'd be much obliged if they'd have him put away, same as the woman he murdered, in the old kit-bag.'

'What time – did he do it?' asked Johnson.

'Ten o'clock last night, sir, the warder says.'

Jerry Bundler

W. W. Jacobs

It wanted a few nights to Christmas, a festival for which the small market town of Torchester was making extensive preparations. The narrow streets which had been thronged with people were now almost deserted; the cheap-jack from London, with the remnant of breath left in him after his evening's exertions, was making feeble attempts to blow out his naphtha lamp, and the last shops open were rapidly closing for the night.

In the comfortable coffee room of the old Boar's Head, half a dozen guests, principally commercial travellers, sat talking by the light of the fire. The talk had drifted from trade to politics, from politics to religion, and so by easy stages to the supernatural. Three ghost stories, never known to fail before, had fallen flat; there was too much noise outside, too much light within. The fourth story was told by an old hand with more success; the streets were quiet, and he had turned the gas out. In the flickering light of the fire, as it shone on the glasses and danced with shadows on the walls, the story proved so enthralling that George, the waiter, whose presence had been forgotten, created a very disagreeable sensation by suddenly starting up from a dark corner and gliding silently from the room. 'That's what I call a good story,' said one of the men, sipping his hot whisky. 'Of course it's an old idea that spirits like to get into the company of human beings. A man told me once that he travelled down the Great Western with a ghost and hadn't the slightest suspicion of it until the inspector came for tickets. My friend said the way that ghost tried to keep up appearances by feeling for it in all its pockets and looking on the floor – was quite touching. Ultimately it gave it up and with a faint groan vanished through the ventilator.'

'That'll do, Hirst,' said another man.

'It's not a subject for jesting,' said a little old gentleman who had been an attentive listener. 'I've never seen an apparition myself, but I know people who have, and I consider that they form a very interesting link between us and the afterlife. There's a ghost story connected with this house, you know.'

'Never heard of it,' said another speaker, 'and I've been here some years now.'

'It dates back a long time now,' said the old gentleman. 'You've heard about Jerry Bundler, George?'

'Well, I've just 'eard odds and ends, sir,' said the old waiter, 'but I never put much count to 'em. There was one chap 'ere what said 'e saw it, and the gov'ner sacked 'im prompt.'

'My father was a native of this town,' said the old

gentleman, 'and knew the story well. He was a truthful man and a steady churchgoer, but I've heard him declare that once in his life he saw the appearance of Jerry Bundler in this house.'

'And who was this Bundler?' inquired a voice.

'A London thief, pickpocket, highwayman – anything he could turn his dishonest hand to,' replied the old gentleman; 'and he was run to earth in this house one Christmas week some eighty years ago. He took his last supper in this very room, and after he had gone up to bed a couple of Bow Street runners, who had followed him from London but lost the scent a bit, went upstairs with the landlord and tried the door. It was stout oak, and fast, so one went into the yard, and by means of a short ladder got onto the windowsill, while the other stayed outside the door. Those below in the yard saw the man crouching on the sill, and then there was a sudden smash of glass, and with a cry he fell in a heap on the stones at their feet. Then in the moonlight they saw the white face of the pickpocket peeping over the sill, and while some stayed in the yard, others ran into the house and helped the other man to break the door in. It was difficult to obtain an entrance even then, for it was barred with heavy furniture, but they got in at last, and the first thing that met their eyes was the body of Jerry dangling from the top of the bed by his own handkerchief.'

'Which bedroom was it?' asked two or three voices together.

The narrator shook his head. 'That I can't tell you; but the story goes that Jerry still haunts this house, and my father used to declare positively that the last time he slept here the ghost of Jerry Bundler lowered itself from the top of his bed and tried to strangle him.'

'That'll do,' said an uneasy voice. 'I wish you'd thought to ask your father which bedroom it was.'

'What for?' inquired the old gentleman.

'Well, I should take care not to sleep in it, that's all,' said the voice, shortly.

'There's nothing to fear,' said the other. 'I don't believe for a moment that ghosts could really hurt one. In fact my father used to confess that it was only the unpleasantness of the thing that upset him, and that for all practical purposes Jerry's fingers might have been made of cotton wool for all the harm they could do.'

'That's all very fine,' said the last speaker again; 'a ghost story is a ghost story, sir; but when a gentleman tells a tale of a ghost in the house in which one is going to sleep, I call it most ungentlemanly!'

'Pooh! Nonsense!' said the old gentleman, rising; 'ghosts can't hurt you. For my own part, I should rather like to see one. Good night, gentlemen.'

'Good night,' said the others. 'And I only hope Jerry'll pay you a visit,' added the nervous man as the door closed.

'Bring some more whisky, George,' said a stout commercial; 'I want keeping up when the talk turns this way.'

'Shall I light the gas, Mr Malcolm?' said George.

'No; the fire's very comfortable,' said the traveller. 'Now, gentlemen, any of you know any more?'

'I think we've had enough,' said another man; 'we shall be thinking we see spirits next, and we're not all like the old gentleman who's just gone.'

'Old humbug!' said Hirst. 'I should like to put him to the test. Suppose I dress up as Jerry Bundler and go and give him a chance of displaying his courage?'

'Bravo!' said Malcolm, huskily, drowning one or two faint 'Nos'. 'Just for the joke, gentlemen.'

'No, no! Drop it, Hirst,' said another man.

'Only for the joke,' said Hirst, somewhat eagerly. 'I've got some things upstairs in which I am going to play in the Rivals – knee-breeches, buckles and all that sort of thing. It's a rare chance. If you'll wait a bit I'll give you a full dress rehearsal, entitled, "Jerry Bundler; or, The Nocturnal Strangler".'

'You won't frighten us,' said the commercial, with a husky laugh.

'I don't know that,' said Hirst, sharply; 'it's a question of acting, that's all. I'm pretty good, ain't I, Somers?'

'Oh, you're all right – for an amateur,' said his friend, with a laugh.

'I'll bet you a level sovereign you don't frighten me,' said the stout traveller.

'Done!' said Hirst. 'I'll take the bet to frighten you first and the old gentleman afterwards. These gentlemen shall be the judges.'

'You won't frighten us, sir,' said another man, 'because we're prepared for you; but you'd better leave the old man alone. It's dangerous play.'

'Well, I'll try you first,' said Hirst, springing up. 'No gas, mind.'

He ran lightly upstairs to his room, leaving the others, most of whom had been drinking somewhat freely, to wrangle about his proceedings. It ended in two of them going to bed.

'He's crazy on acting,' said Somers, lighting his pipe. 'Thinks he's the equal of anybody almost. It doesn't matter with us, but I won't let him go to the old man. And he won't mind so long as he gets an opportunity of acting to us.'

'Well, I hope he'll hurry up,' said Malcolm, yawning; 'it's after twelve now.'

Nearly half an hour passed. Malcolm drew his watch from his pocket and was busy winding it, when George, the waiter, who had been sent on an errand to the bar, burst suddenly into the room and rushed towards them.

''E's comin', gentlemen,' he said breathlessly.

'Why, you're frightened, George,' said the stout commercial, with a chuckle.

'It was the suddenness of it,' said George, sheepishly; 'and besides, I didn't look for seein' 'im in the bar. There's only a glimmer of light there, and 'e was sitting on the floor behind the bar. I nearly trod on 'im.'

'Oh, you'll never make a man, George,' said Malcolm.

'Well, it took me unawares,' said the waiter. 'Not that I'd have gone to the bar by myself if I'd known 'e was there, and I don't believe you would either, sir.'

'Nonsense!' said Malcolm. 'I'll go and fetch him in.'

'You don't know what it's like, sir,' said George, catching him by the sleeve. 'It ain't fit to look at by yourself, it ain't, indeed. It's got the – what's that?'

They all started at the sound of a smothered cry from the staircase and the sound of somebody running hurriedly along the passage. Before anybody could speak, the door flew open and a figure bursting into the room flung itself gasping and shivering upon them.

'What is it? What's the matter?' demanded Malcolm. 'Why, it's Mr Hirst.' He shook him roughly and then held some spirit to his lips. Hirst drank it greedily and with a sharp intake of his breath gripped him by the arm.

'Light the gas, George,' said Malcolm.

The waiter obeyed hastily. Hirst, a ludicrous but pitiable figure in knee-breeches and coat, a large wig all awry and his face a mess of grease paint, clung to him, trembling.

'Now, what's the matter?' asked Malcolm.

'I've seen it,' said Hirst, with a hysterical sob. 'O Lord, I'll never play the fool again, never!'

'Seen what?' said the others.

'Him – it – the ghost – anything!' said Hirst, wildly.

'Rot!' said Malcolm, uneasily.

'I was coming down the stairs,' said Hirst. 'Just capering down – as I thought – it ought to do. I felt a tap—'

He broke off suddenly and peered nervously through the open door into the passage.

'I thought I saw it again,' he whispered.

'Look – at the foot of the stairs. Can you see anything?'

'No, there's nothing there,' said Malcolm, whose own voice shook a little. 'Go on. You felt a tap on your shoulder—'

'I turned round and saw it – a little wicked head and a white dead face. Pah!'

'That's what I saw in the bar,' said George. ''Orrid it was – devilish!'

Hirst shuddered, and, still retaining his nervous grip of Malcolm's sleeve, dropped into a chair.

'Well, it's a most unaccountable thing,' said the

dumbfounded Malcolm, turning round to the others. 'It's the last time I come to this house.'

'I leave tomorrow,' said George. 'I wouldn't go down to that bar again by myself, no, not for fifty pounds!'

'It's talking about the thing that's caused it, I expect,' said one of the men; 'we've all been talking about this and having it in our minds. Practically we've been forming a spiritualistic circle without knowing it.'

'Hang the old gentleman!' said Malcolm, heartily. 'Upon my soul, I'm half afraid to go to bed. It's odd they should both think they saw something.'

'I saw it as plain as I see you, sir,' said George, solemnly. 'P'raps if you keep your eyes turned up the passage you'll see it for yourself.'

They followed the direction of his finger, but saw nothing, although one of them fancied that a head peeped round the corner of the wall.

'Who'll come down to the bar?' said Malcolm, looking round.

'You can go, if you like,' said one of the others, with a faint laugh; 'we'll wait here for you.'

The stout traveller walked towards the door and took a few steps up the passage. Then he stopped. All was quite silent, and he walked slowly to the end and looked down fearfully towards the glass partition which shut off the bar. Three times he made as though to go to it; then he turned back, and, glancing over his shoulder, came hurriedly back to the room.

'Did you see it, sir?' whispered George.

'Don't know,' said Malcolm, shortly. 'I fancied I saw

something, but it might have been fancy. I'm in the mood to see anything just now. How are you feeling now, sir?'

'Oh, I feel a bit better now,' said Hirst, somewhat brusquely, as all eyes were turned upon him.

'I dare say you think I'm easily scared, but you didn't see it.'

'Not at all,' said Malcolm, smiling faintly despite himself.

'I'm going to bed,' said Hirst, noticing the smile and resenting it. 'Will you share my room with me, Somers?'

'I will with pleasure,' said his friend, 'provided you don't mind sleeping with the gas on full all night.'

He rose from his seat, and bidding the company a friendly good night, left the room with his crestfallen friend. The others saw them to the foot of the stairs, and having heard their door close, returned to the coffee room.

'Well, I suppose the bet's off?' said the stout commercial, poking the fire and then standing with his legs apart on the hearthrug; 'though, as far as I can see, I won it. I never saw a man so scared in all my life. Sort of poetic justice about it, isn't there?'

'Never mind about poetry or justice,' said one of his listeners; 'who's going to sleep with me?'

'I will,' said Malcolm, affably.

'And I suppose we share a room together, Mr Leek?' said the third man, turning to the fourth.

'No, thank you,' said the other, briskly; 'I don't believe in ghosts. If anything comes into my room I shall shoot it.'

'That won't hurt a spirit, Leek,' said Malcolm, decisively.

'Well the noise'll be like company to me,' said Leek, 'and it'll wake the house too. But if you're nervous, sir,' he added, with a grin, to the man who had suggested sharing his room, 'George'll be only too pleased to sleep on the doormat inside your room, I know.'

'That I will, sir,' said George, fervently; 'and if you gentlemen would only come down with me to the bar to put the gas out, I could never be sufficiently grateful.'

They went out in a body, with the exception of Leek, peering carefully before them as they went. George turned the light out in the bar and they returned unmolested to the coffee room, and, avoiding the sardonic smile of Leek, prepared to separate for the night.

'Give me the candle while you put the gas out, George,' said the traveller.

The waiter handed it to him and extinguished the gas, and at the same moment all distinctly heard a step in the passage outside. It stopped at the door, and as they watched with bated breath, the door creaked and slowly opened. Malcolm fell back open-mouthed, as a white, leering face, with sunken eyeballs and close-cropped bullet head, appeared at the opening.

For a few seconds the creature stood regarding them, blinking in a strange fashion at the candle. Then, with a sidling movement, it came a little way into the room and stood there as if bewildered.

Not a man spoke or moved, but all watched with a horrible fascination as the creature removed its dirty neckcloth and its head rolled on its shoulder. For a minute it paused, and then, holding the rag before it, moved towards Malcolm.

The candle went out suddenly with a flash and a bang. There was a smell of powder, and something writhing in the darkness on the floor. A faint, choking cough, and then silence. Malcolm was the first to speak. 'Matches,' he said, in a strange voice. George struck one. Then he leapt at the gas and a burner flamed from the match. Malcolm touched the thing on the floor with his foot and found it soft. He looked at his companions. They mouthed inquiries at him, but he shook his head. He lit the candle, and, kneeling down, examined the silent thing on the floor. Then he rose swiftly, and dipping his handkerchief in the water jug, bent down again and grimly wiped the white face. Then he sprang back with a cry of incredulous horror, pointing at it. Leek's pistol fell to the floor and he shut out the sight with his hands, but the others, crowding forward, gazed spell-bound at the dead face of Hirst.

Before a word was spoken the door opened and Somers hastily entered the room. His eyes fell on the floor. 'Good God!' he cried. 'You didn't—'

Nobody spoke.

'I told him not to,' he said, in a suffocating voice. 'I told him not to. I told him—'

He leaned against the wall, deathly sick, put his arms out feebly, and fell fainting into the traveller's arms.

Credits

'A Pair of Muddy Shoes' by Lennox Robinson © Lennox Robinson Estate held by the Abbey Theatre Amharclann na Mainistreach

'The Book' by Margaret Irwin is reprinted by permission of Peters, Fraser and Dunlop (www.petersfraserdunlop.com) on behalf of Rights Limited

'A Bad Heart' by Ruth Rendell from the collection The Fallen Curtain and Other Stories © Kingsmarkham Enterprises Ltd, 1982, is reprinted with permission from United Agents

While every effort has been made to contact copyright-holders of each story, the editor and publishers would be grateful for information where they have been unable to trace them, and would be glad to make amendments in further editions.